A Thief in the Night . . .

"What the . . . !"

Longarm came upright off his bedroll, on his feet with his .45 in hand before he consciously realized that he was awake.

Someone was trying to steal his horse. The moon was not yet up, so it must have been early in the night, but by the dim light of a crisply cold Milky Way he could see a pale figure trying to get the hobbles off the animal.

Longarm did not hesitate. Horse stealing was still a hanging offense in Colorado, and he had always thought that 255 grains of .45-caliber lead were the equivalent of a hangman's noose.

He took careful aim, so as to avoid hitting his own animal, and triggered off a shot.

The thief crumpled to the rocky ground, hit somewhere in the back.

Longarm rushed forward, ready to fire again if the son of a bitch offered to shoot back. He knelt beside the would-be thief.

And cursed aloud.

The person who was trying to steal his horse was a woman . . .

TABOR EVANS

LONGARM

AND THE HORSE THIEF'S DAUGHTER

JOVE BOOKS, NEW YORK

THE BERKLEY PUBLISHING GROUP
Published by the Penguin Group
Penguin Group (USA)
375 Hudson Street, New York, New York 10014, USA

USA I Canada I UK I Ireland I Australia I New Zealand I India I South Africa I China

Penguin Books Ltd., Registered Offices: 80 Strand, London WC2R 0RL, England
For more information about the Penguin Group, visit penguin.com.

LONGARM AND THE HORSE THIEF'S DAUGHTER

A Jove Book / published by arrangement with the author

Jove Books are published by The Berkley Publishing Group.
JOVE® is a registered trademark of Penguin Group (USA).
The "J" design is a trademark of Penguin Group (USA).

For information, address: The Berkley Publishing Group,
a division of Penguin Group (USA),
375 Hudson Street, New York, New York 10014.

ISBN: 978-0-515-15377-4

PUBLISHING HISTORY
Jove mass-market edition / September 2013

PRINTED IN THE UNITED STATES OF AMERICA

10 9 8 7 6 5 4 3 2 1

Cover illustration by Milo Sinovcic.

This is a work of fiction. Names, characters, places, and incidents either are the product
of the author's imagination or are used fictitiously, and any resemblance to actual persons,
living or dead, business establishments, events, or locales is entirely coincidental.
The publisher does not have any control over and does not assume any responsibility for
author or third-party websites or their content.

ALWAYS LEARNING   **PEARSON**

Chapter 1

Deputy United States Marshal Custis Long leaned back, crossed his legs, and lighted a cheroot. "Just think, Boss. This time next week I'll be somewhere up in them mountains with my gear laid out beside one o' them little lakes, a fresh-caught trout sizzlin' in the pan, and a pot o' coffee on the coals. I'm telling you, Billy, that's the life. I'm looking forward to it. First real vacation I'll've had in . . . I don't even know how long."

Chief Marshal William Vail smiled. "Do you want me to look it up and find out how long it has been?"

"Uh, thanks for the offer, but I reckon I don't really need to know." Longarm puffed on his cheroot and blew a series of smoke rings into the air between him and Billy.

"Is there anything you want me to do before I head out?" he asked.

"Thanks for asking, but no. You are free to go."

Longarm grinned and stood, rising to his full height of more than six feet. He was an impressive figure of a man, with broad shoulders, a narrow waist, and long legs. He had brown hair and a sweeping, brown handlebar mustache. His face was leathery, deeply tanned by years on horseback. He considered himself ordinary, perhaps even homely, but women seemed to find him more than passingly handsome.

He wore a brown checked tweed coat, brown corduroy trousers, and black stovepipe boots. A black leather gunbelt cinched his middle with a double-action .45 Colt carried in a cross-draw holster. A watch chain stretched across his belly from one vest pocket to the other. One end of the chain was attached to an Ingersoll railroad grade watch, but the other held a .41-caliber derringer, useful in some situations.

In his inside coat pocket was a folded leather wallet, inside of which was his badge. That too was useful in certain circumstances.

At the moment Longarm's thoughts were not on the dangers of his job but on the pleasures of getting away from it.

"You're sure you don't need nothing, Boss?" he asked.

"Dammit, Long, I know what I need, and right now what I require is that you go on about your vacation. I have work to do right here." Billy shook his head, his bald dome catching the light spilling through the window at his back. "I'll be lucky to get out of the office before midnight tonight, so go on and let me get to it.

The chief marshal sighed. "If I had known how much pencil pushing and paper shuffling was involved with this job, I think I would have turned it down. So please. Leave. Go catch a fish or . . . something." Billy waved a hand as if shooing an annoying housefly.

"Right, Boss. Then I'll, um, I'll see you in three weeks."

Vail made the shooing motion again and bent to the papers laid out on his desk.

Longarm stood and silently slipped out of the marshal's office.

He crossed Cherry Creek to his boardinghouse to finish packing. When he was done with that, he removed his city clothes, keeping only his duds from the waist down but leaving the tweed coat, the vest with its watch chain, and the derringer—after all, a man on vacation does not need a watch—and substituting a much worn and battered version of his brand-new snuff-brown Stetson hat.

He collected a blanket-lined canvas coat from his wardrobe—it could be cold in the mountains at any time of year—and added a sheepskin vest. The vest he pulled on immediately; the coat he bundled together and strapped to the outside of his travel-worn carpetbag.

He removed his bedroll from the cantle of his ball-busting McClellan saddle, figuring that while on vacation he would value comfort for himself more than for any rented horse he might find himself using. Beside, he would not be pushing an animal up there in the mountains. There would be no need for the saddle. This would be a quiet, leisurely sort of vacation. Nothing exciting at all.

Longarm started yawning and relaxing even before he left the boardinghouse and stepped down into the street in search of a hansom to carry him and his gear to the railroad depot.

Peace and quiet were just exactly what he needed, he thought. And what he intended to have.

But then the best laid plans can come apart.

Chapter 2

Longarm had to actually pay for a train ticket this trip. It felt odd to break out his wallet for a change. When he did, the ticket agent saw his badge and asked, "Are you a marshal, mister?"

"A deputy, yes," Longarm told him.

"You know that U.S. marshals ride free, don't you? It's part of the agreement because we carry the mail. We have to provide certain services to you government boys."

Longarm smiled at the young man. "Oh, I know that all right, an' I'd ride on the badge if I was on official business. This time, though, I'm on my own." His smile widened into a grin. "Vacation, don't you see. First one in quite a while."

"Silver Plume seems a strange place to go for a vacation," the clerk said. "It's kind of smoky and it smells of chemicals, and of course there is all the noise from those stamp mills pounding rock into dust. No, sir, it just seems strange that a man would go there for vacation."

"It is all of that," Longarm agreed, "but it's a good jumping-off place if you want t' get up into the mountains. Which I do. Got me a brand-new fly rod. Split bamboo all the way from God-knows-where. And I've been tying flies in my spare time for the past month." He laughed. "Such spare time as I have, which ain't much, but I got me a mess o' flies that I figure to exchange for a mess o' fish once I get up there. I'm really lookin' forward to this here trip."

"I don't blame you at all, Marshal. Let's see. Denver to Silver Plume . . . that will be seven dollars and sixty-five cents."

Longarm whistled. "Lordy. So much?"

"If you want to show me that badge again, you can ride for free," the clerk offered.

Longarm shook his head. "No, sir, I'm not gonna take advantage like that. Wouldn't be right."

"In that case, it's seven dollars and. . . ."

"I know. I heard you the first time. I just didn't realize that you railroad folks are such robbers. Seems like I oughta be arrestin' you for highway robbery."

But he dug out his pocket purse and handed the man a ten-dollar gold eagle fresh from the mint across the street from the Federal Building, where Billy Vail had his offices. The clerk made the appropriate change and handed it to him along with the ticket to Silver Plume.

Longarm lugged his own gear to the baggage car rather than pay a porter to do that job for him; then he walked forward to the second of the two passenger coaches.

There were only a handful of passengers going up into the mining district; consequently there was no lounge car attached to this train and no opportunity for a card game to pass the time en route. Longarm selected a seat by a window. He shoved the window up and hoped there would be no cinders blowing in through it. Not that his camping clothes were so precious that a cinder burn would do any harm. Or even be noticed.

With time to kill and no plan in mind, Longarm smoked a cheroot while he waited for the train to pull out of the station. When he was done with his smoke, he flicked the butt out of the open window, slumped down low in his seat, and tugged his hat brim low over his eyes. He might just as well start relaxing right here and now, he decided, and he closed his eyes to take a nap, visions of huge trout in his thoughts.

Chapter 3

The train slowed with a shudder and a crashing of couplings. Finally it came to a jolting halt, and the conductor, a pudgy man in a scarlet coat and flat cap, announced, "Silver Plume, all out for Silver Plume."

Longarm was the only passenger detraining at the Silver Plume station. He stepped down onto the platform, the air full of the stink of coal smoke and steam, the engine hissing and snorting like something that belonged in Hell itself.

He walked back to the baggage car and retrieved his gear and carried everything across the street and down several blocks to the livery.

"Why, hello, Marshal," the hostler said in greeting.

Longarm remembered the man from a previous visit but could not recall his name. He smiled and said, "Howdy. It's good t' see you again."

"Good to see you too, Marshal. What will you be wanting this trip?"

"A decent riding animal, with tack, and a mule or a burro to carry my things here," Longarm told him.

"I have just what you need. Count on it. Will this be on a government voucher like the last time, Marshal?"

Longarm sighed. "No, this is out of my own pocket, so go easy on me, will you?"

The hostler lifted an eyebrow but did not question the change. "I'll give you my best rate. Fifty cents a day for the horse and a quarter for a sturdy little burro I got out back. And I'll throw in the tack for the horse and a pack saddle for the burro. I can't do fairer than that."

Longarm paused for a moment to work out what three weeks in the mountains would cost. It was a good deal the man was offering. He nodded and produced a twenty-dollar double eagle that he handed to the man, saying, "There should be some change from that, but we'll figure that out when I get back from wherever I end up."

The hostler—his name was Eugene, Longarm remembered now—slipped the gold coin into his pocket. "You're headed up the mountain, I take it. Prospecting?"

"Fishing," Longarm told him.

Eugene nodded. "There's nothing on this side of the mountain, but over on t'other side there's some good lakes for fishing and some decent streams feeding them. They say the trout practically jump into your frying pan and ask to be et."

"I hope you're right about that," Longarm said. "It sounds like just what I need."

"Do you want I should cut them out and saddle them for you?" Eugene asked.

"No," Longarm said, "I'm in no hurry. I think tonight I'll spend in a bed. Maybe play some cards if I can find a game." He grinned again. "An' eat somebody else's cooking one last time before I sour my gut with my own cooking for the next few weeks."

Eugene laughed. "If I had to eat my own cooking, Marshal, I'd starve. Or poison myself. Tomorrow morning early, then?"

"That sounds about right, Eugene. Crack o' dawn. Or, um, anyway before noon."

"They'll be ready for you. If you'd like to leave your gear here, I'll have it all loaded for you."

"That's mighty nice o' you. Thanks."

"Glad to be of service, Marshal."

"In that case, Gene, I'll see you in the morning." Longarm touched the brim of his Stetson and ambled out of the livery.

There was a boardinghouse just a block away, one that he remembered from his last visit to Silver Plume.

He just hoped that the same little widow woman, Mrs. Amanda Carricker, was still running the place.

Chapter 4

Amanda greeted him with a huge smile and a warm hug. "Custis. What a nice surprise. Will you be staying with me for a spell?"

"Just for one night, Mandy." He laughed. "I don't think I could handle more'n that."

"I would like to test that claim," she said, leading him into the foyer.

Carricker's Boarding was a three-story house. Paying boarders had the top two floors, while Amanda lived in an addition built behind the kitchen.

"Do you have a room for me?" Longarm asked.

"Dear," Amanda said, linking her arm into his, "you will be staying down here with me." She winked and added, "Of course, my sweet."

He gave the lady a kiss on the forehead and leaned back to look her over. She had changed little since the last time he saw her.

Longarm had never asked, but he guessed that the widow was in her early forties or thereabouts.

She was a small woman, vivacious and happy. She had black hair pinned up in a severe bun at the back of her head, dark eyes, full lips, and a diminutive height but a full—and then some—figure.

Amanda ran a very efficient boardinghouse, with boarders fed well at her serving table morning and evening alike.

And the lady liked to fuck.

Longarm felt her tongue slide into his mouth and her hand grope his cock.

She stepped back from him and winked again. "Later, dear. After my duties are done."

She led him into the parlor and got him settled into a comfortable chair, then disappeared into the kitchen. Moments later a tall woman emerged from that same door, this lady carrying a tray with a bottle of brandy and snifters.

Longarm jumped to his feet. "Ma'am."

She smiled. "I'm LouAnne," she said. "Amanda and I were roommates at finishing school. Now we live much too far apart, so I am here for a visit."

That put LouAnne at about the same age as Amanda, but physically the two could not have been much more different. LouAnne was tall and slim and elegant. She had dark auburn hair and green eyes, apple cheeks and long, long eyelashes.

"Brandy?" she offered.

"Sure."

LouAnne poured the brandy and handed the balloon glass to Longarm. He remembered how a gentleman was supposed to handle the drink—although he preferred less fuss and more kick—so he stuck his nose above the bell of the brandy snifter and inhaled.

Not that he knew what all the fuss was supposed to be about. Booze was booze and the idea was to drink it, not to sniff it.

Still, it was all a matter of politeness, he supposed. He saluted LouAnne with his glass and took a swig. For brandy this was not bad stuff.

"Another?" Mandy's old friend offered.

"Sure, why not."

"Dinner will be served promptly at six, then the gentlemen will retire either to the parlor or to the porch. Mandy suggests you might like to join the two of us in her suite," LouAnne said.

Longarm nodded and took a small sip—he had guzzled the first glass, forgetting that brandy drinkers were supposed to go slow with their drinking for some reason—then said, "It'll be my pleasure."

When LouAnne bent down to serve the brandy, he could not help but notice that the lady had practically nothing inside the bodice of her gown. She just about had no tits.

Not that that mattered. But she was otherwise a rather attractive woman.

None of his business, of course. She was just Mandy's old pal, probably married and with a passel of children back wherever it was that she came from.

"Six, you said," he said, regretting that he'd left his watch back home. He was getting hungry.

"Can I get you something to tide you over?"

Longarm grinned. "You, lady, are a mind reader. Thanks."

"Make yourself comfortable there." She laughed. "You will know when it is time for dinner. There will be a stampede for the dining room that you won't be able to miss."

Longarm saluted the lady with his snifter again and reached for the brandy decanter to help himself to another. It seemed the more he drank of this shit the better he liked it.

Chapter 5

They left LouAnne in the parlor chatting with some of the gentlemen who boarded with Amanda. Longarm and his gracious hostess retired to her suite, which consisted of a small sitting room where she could escape to some privacy and a much larger and comfortably furnished bedroom.

Amanda shed her clothing with a magician's speed. Longarm grinned and shucked his as well.

He had long heard the expression that anything more than a mouthful was wasted, but he had to admire tits as large as Mandy's. They were as big as ripe melons with nipples the size of a workingman's thumb. He happened to know from past experience that those nipples were marvelously sensitive.

Her tits were beginning to sag as middle age set in, but her waist was still small, her belly reasonably flat, and her legs shapely. Her bush was black and tightly curled.

He took her into his arms and kissed her, then allowed her—it was awfully nice of him—to lead him to the bed.

"Wait," she said. Amanda turned and drew the bedspread down. Longarm thought the rear view was quite as nice as the front of her. Her butt was round and pink, and he happened to know that she liked to be fucked there.

When she straightened up, he wrapped his arms around her, his now throbbingly erect cock fitting nicely into the crack of her ass, and kissed her on the back of the neck.

Amanda shivered and guided his hands to her tits. He toyed with her nipples. This time she shuddered with a sudden convulsive climax. He had forgotten how easily the lady came, but he liked it. A woman who reached her climax that quickly was a pleasure, made a man feel like quite the accomplished lover, never mind that it was her sensitivity and not his expertise that made the difference.

Longarm turned her around and kissed her again. While their mouths were locked together, their tongues probing and fencing, he picked her up and placed her down onto the sheets.

"Don't come inside yet," Mandy warned. "I want you nice and fresh while I suck you for a while first. And if you don't mind, I would like for you to suck me too."

"I don't mind a bit," Longarm whispered into her ear.

Amanda laughed. "That tickles."

"Good." He did it again, and she shivered. He was not sure if she had come again or not, so he did it a third time. This time he was sure. She reached another climax.

He dipped his head to her tits and began to suck her right nipple.

"Wait," Amanda said. She wriggled around beneath him so that her head was at his crotch while his nose was buried in her bush. "Now," she said.

She peeled back his foreskin and took him into her mouth, engulfing him in wet heat.

"Damn that feels good," he said.

"Shut up and lick me," Amanda demanded.

He did as he was asked, and the woman shuddered again, her pussy clenching tight and practically asking for a dick to be placed there.

In good time, he thought. That was one of the advantages

of starting early. They had plenty of time to play and explore and enjoy.

Longarm's nose was buried in Amanda's pussy when he heard the unmistakable click of a door latch being opened. And him caught naked as a boiled egg with his face buried in Amanda Carricker's short and curlies.

Chapter 6

"Naughty, naughty." And then laughter.

Longarm looked up, fairly well mortified, to see Mandy's old school chum LouAnne standing beside the bed.

"And what are you two doing?" LouAnne said. "As if I didn't know. Shame on you." She laughed. "Shame on you for not inviting me to this party." With that the tall, lovely woman began to strip off her clothing.

LouAnne, it turned out, had a perfectly lovely body, long and sleek and flawless. Flawless, that is, unless you counted an almost complete absence of tits as a flaw.

What passed for tits on LouAnne's scrawny chest were tiny bags of flesh with even smaller pink nipples set atop. Longarm had seen flapjacks with more body than LouAnne's tits.

The rest of her body was well nigh perfect, however. Her belly was completely flat, her waist tiny—Longarm wondered if she might have taken a page from the book of Southern girls who had their lower ribs removed so they could achieve unnaturally small waists—and her legs slim.

She had no pubic hair. None. Her crotch was as naked as the rest of her. Obviously she shaved there, and had done so recently because she had no stubble. Longarm liked the look. She seemed clean and inviting with her pink slit on display.

"Well?" she demanded.

Amanda rolled onto her back and smiled. "Come join us," she invited.

LouAnne did not have to be asked twice. She lay down and began fondling Mandy's tits, then sucking her friend's nipples.

"You don't mind, do you, dear?" Amanda asked.

"I, un, no, of course not," Longarm stammered.

"Good." LouAnne transferred her attentions to Longarm, alternately kissing him and then kissing Amanda's pussy.

She moved toward the foot of the bed and while Longarm ate Amanda's cunt, LouAnne sucked Longarm's cock.

"Tasty," she said at one point, smacking her lips loudly and then laughing.

"Have you come yet, dear?" LouAnne asked.

Longarm was not sure which of them the question was intended for, but Amanda answered, "Not yet, sweetie."

"Let me know when you do."

A minute or so later Amanda shuddered and moaned and shortly afterward said, "Oh, yes, I did."

"Then let's switch," LouAnne said. "I want to taste that sweet pussy juice."

Longarm lay on his back while the girls exchanged places, Amanda going down on his rock-hard cock while Longarm had the distinct pleasure of eating LouAnne's clean and smooth and lightly perfumed pussy.

"Both now," LouAnne said after several minutes.

Longarm did not know what the two women intended. He had no complaints when he found out. Both of them concentrated on his middle, Amanda sucking his cock while LouAnne licked and sucked his balls.

They rolled him onto his side, and laughing playfully, the two moved one in front and the other in back, LouAnne sucking Longarm's cock while Amanda tongued his asshole and the sensitive area at the base of his balls.

"Unless you want . . . ," he began, then, "Oh, never mind."

He let go, releasing his load of cum into a mouth. At that point he was not even entirely sure whose mouth he was coming in—it turned out to be LouAnne's—and he did not much care. Whoever it was felt damned good deep in her mouth.

The girls sat up laughing and wiping their mouths.

"Switch now," Amanda said.

"Again?" Longarm asked.

"Oh, I think you will like this, dear."

"I've damn sure liked it so far, so just tell me what you have in mind."

What Amanda intended became clear soon enough. Amanda sucked Longarm while Longarm sucked LouAnne while LouAnne sucked Amanda.

"The way we play," Amanda explained helpfully, "is that we stay like this until everyone has had a chance to come." She giggled. "Then we switch around and everybody swaps."

"That's when I get to drink your cum," LouAnne said.

"And I get to eat Annie's pussy," Amanda added.

"See? Now, come on. It will be fun."

It was fun indeed.

Chapter 7

Longarm ate an early breakfast at the kitchen table. He did not want to show himself in the dining room lest he confuse the paying boarders, who did not have kitchen—or bed—privileges.

It was still dark when he slipped out the back door and made his way back to the livery. Early as it was, the liveryman was awake and busy with his animals.

"You're ready to go? Give me a few minutes and I'll have you loaded for the trail," the liveryman said. He smiled. "I wasn't expecting you quite so early. Sorry."

"No need to apologize, Eugene," Longarm told him. "My plans . . ." He laughed, then said, "I don't have any plans, actually. Feels strange for a change."

He checked the loading, but Eugene knew his business and did a more than competent job of getting Longarm's saddle and packs secured in place. Longarm just hoped he could get everything back the way it was supposed to be after he broke the packs down come evening.

That, however, would be hours and miles away from Silver Plume. And from Amanda.

Longarm smiled, thinking of her. And her girlhood friend LouAnne. They were quite a pair.

He wondered if he was going to have to stop somewhere this afternoon and take a nap. He damn sure had not gotten much sleep during the night.

"You're all set," Eugene said just as the sky was beginning to grow pale toward the east.

The hostler had chosen a sturdy, brown mare for Longarm's mount and a fuzzy-eared burro to carry the packs. The saddle on the brown was wide and comfortable, unlike the army-style McClellan ball-buster Longarm usually rode.

He almost felt guilty about granting himself so much comfort. Almost. He was on vacation, wasn't he? He *deserved* a little time away to fish and loaf and relax.

He stepped up onto that very comfortable saddle and smiled. It felt good for a change.

"Thanks, Eugene. Don't look for me to be back for a couple, three weeks or so. I figure to be up in the high country enjoying life."

"Wish I could go with you, Marshal."

"Next time maybe you can," Longarm said, not meaning it but wanting to be polite. He touched the brim of his Stetson and let the mare walk out of the barn, the burro following docilely behind on a cotton lead rope.

It was good to be on vacation, he thought.

Chapter 8

A narrow switchback trail led north from Silver Plume, probably an old game trail widened and put into use by prospectors seeking the precious metals that made Colorado such an integral part of the nation's economy, and by the freighters and miners who came after them.

Longarm made his way slowly up the south slope of the mountain that loomed above Amanda's boardinghouse. He was in no hurry. After all, he was on vacation.

He passed only one other outfit, a short string of very large mules that were on their way down the same trail. Longarm tried to be sociable, but the muleskinner was in no humor for pleasantries. The man barely grunted an acknowledgment of Longarm's presence after Longarm politely pulled off on the side of the trail to allow the mules to pass. Then man and mules were gone, and Longarm was left with no company save his own animals and a hawk riding high overhead on some unseen air current.

Noontime found Longarm midway up the mountain. He paused for a cold lunch of hardtack and jerky and a swallow of tepid water from his canteen, then continued on hoping that the damn trout were worth all this.

Dusk came just as he crested the mountaintop. The view

was fabulous, even by Colorado standards. Tall mountains and deep canyons surrounded him, and the cold, crisp air reached deep into his lungs. It seemed to please his soul as much as it did his body, and he dismounted to stand and admire.

If there were any church or cathedral as grand as this, he reckoned, he would be a regular attendee.

Standing and ogling was not accomplishing anything, though. He quickly stripped both horse and burro of the burdens they had carried all day long. He hobbled the animals and turned them loose to forage a meal for themselves while he added some rocks to a firepit that others before him had used up here.

He collected some reasonably dry deadwood and built a small fire. He poured enough water into his pot to make two cups of coffee, one for tonight and the other to be saved for morning, and gave the rest of his water to the animals.

Come morning he would need to find that fishing lake or mountain stream, if only to provide water for himself and the animals.

He mixed some dough with flour, lard, and salt and wrapped it around a stick that he used to roast the dough over the side of the fire while the coffee water was boiling.

"This is the life, eh?" he said aloud to the grazing horse and burro. Neither responded, so Longarm sat and shivered in the evening chill. He thought about getting up and digging his coat out of the packs, then decided that would be too much work. It was easier to sit in the flickering glow of the firelight and shiver.

Within minutes of finishing his meal, such as it was, he spread his bedroll and lay down to an overdue sleep. He was so tired he was almost glad that neither Amanda nor LouAnne was here with him.

Chapter 9

"What the . . . !"

Longarm came upright off his bedroll, on his feet with his .45 in hand before he consciously realized that he was awake.

Someone was trying to steal his horse. The moon was not yet up, so it must have been early in the night, but by the dim light of a crisply cold Milky Way he could see a pale figure trying to get the hobbles off the animal.

Longarm did not hesitate. Horse stealing was still a hanging offense in Colorado, and he had always thought that 255 grains of .45-caliber lead were the equivalent of a hangman's noose.

He took careful aim, so as to avoid hitting his own animal, and triggered off a shot.

The thief crumpled to the rocky ground, hit somewhere in the back.

Longarm rushed forward, ready to fire again if the son of a bitch offered to shoot back. He knelt beside the would-be thief.

And cursed aloud.

The person who was trying to steal his horse was a woman. He knew that for certain sure because she was wearing a flimsy sort of nightgown and had hair down to her butt.

She might have been pretty or homely, he had no idea. There was not enough light for him to see her that well. But one thing he was sure of was that his bullet had found its mark. She was bleeding, although not heavily.

He leaned close and thought he could hear ragged, rasping breathing that would suggest he had hit her through a lung.

People can survive a punctured lung. Sometimes. They might also simply lie down and die instead. If she did . . . Longarm would have no regrets. The woman had been trying to steal his horse. The shooting was justified. He had no doubt that a jury would see it that way.

On the other hand, he did not want this woman to die. He would save her if he could.

He picked her up—she seemed to weigh next to nothing—and carried her to his bedroll and placed her on it. Then he fumbled around for the wood he had laid ready for morning and rekindled his fire, building it up high so he could get a better look at her and her wound.

Even with the firelight it took him some time to figure out the maze of buttons and ribbons that held her nightdress together in the front, and more time to work it off of her without causing more pain than was absolutely necessary.

It helped that she had passed out. Shock, he assumed. Whatever the reason, she was as limp as a rag doll under his hands.

He stripped the clothes from her, noting in passing that she had a better than merely decent figure and was passingly good to look at. Or would have been if she had not just been shot. As it was. . . .

The bleeding was light. He took a look at the wound as best he could in the uncertain light. His bullet had struck to the side of her spine and penetrated a lung, just as he had suspected. It might well have hit bone. He could not tell that

The bullet hole, when it was exposed, continued to bubble and pulse with the rhythm of her breathing. Longarm considered that to be a good sign. Especially the part about her breathing.

LouAnne had the woman lying facedown on the broad bed, cleaned up but still out cold after the shock of the gunshot.

Amanda returned after ten or fifteen minutes, a young doctor and his bag of potions and medical gadgets in tow.

"All three of you clear out now," the doctor ordered. "Let me see what we have here."

Longarm turned to go immediately; Amanda and LouAnne were less willing to leave. But then after all, it was their bedroom the unknown woman was inhabiting at the moment.

Longarm went out back to tend to the horse and the burro. Then he came back and slipped inside the bedroom, trying to be silent and unnoticed. By then the doctor was almost done with his examination. He cleaned the bullet hole and applied a plaster to seal it off. The woman immediately began to breathe more easily now that air was no longer leaking through Longarm's makeshift attempt at a seal.

The doctor also put proper bandaging over the plaster and turned the woman onto her back.

He dug a bottle of laudanum out of his bag and set it on the nightstand. "For pain," he said. "When she wakes up . . . if she wakes up . . . she will be in great pain. Give her a few drops of this as needed. All right?"

Amanda and LouAnne both took the instruction seriously. They nodded as one.

"And what are you doing here?" the doctor demanded of Longarm. "I thought I sent you out already. Are you the husband?"

"Doctor, I don't even know who the hell she is. I'm the one that shot her."

"Did you have a good reason?"

"I thought so at the time."

"Good, because I intend to report this to the law."

"Doc, he is the law. Custis here is a deputy United States marshal," Amanda told him.

"He can tell that to the law too. Now, if you will excuse me, I have patients to see." He snapped his bag closed, picked it up, and marched out.

"What will you do now, Custis?" Amanda asked.

"I'd like to hang around a bit and see does she pull through. There's some questions I'd like to ask her. Like for instance what was she doing up on top of that mountain in her nightdress and no sign of a camp or proper clothes. And where was she going with my horse. She wasn't stealing it for money, I wouldn't think. She was wanting to go someplace, and my bullet stopped her from it."

He reached for a cheroot and a match. Once he had the cigar properly alight, he added, "Like I said. I got questions. I figure the answers might be kinda interesting."

"LouAnne, take Custis out into the kitchen and get him some coffee. I'll take over here," Amanda said.

"I could use a bite o' food too. Haven't eaten yet today and I'm kinda hungry."

LouAnne took him by the arm and led him toward the kitchen. "We have some cold pork and nice, crusty bread. Perhaps some coffee too. Would that be all right?"

Chapter 11

"Custis. Wake up."

He opened his eyes to see Amanda bending over him in the dim light of a lamp that was turned down low. He had been dozing in an armchair in her parlor. "Wha time zit?" he mumbled.

"It's about two thirty," she said.

"In the morning?"

"Yes, of course. It wouldn't be this dark at two thirty in the afternoon."

"Oh, um, right." He sat up and rubbed his eyes, continuing the motion to include his whole face. He felt numb. And very tired. At least partially revived, he asked, "What's up?"

"Your victim. She's awake now. I thought you would want to know. You said you wanted to talk with her."

"Right. Thanks." He stood, yawned, and stretched, then followed Amanda through the kitchen to the bedroom. LouAnne was seated in a comfortable chair beside the woman, who now lay propped up on a pair of fluffy pillows. She was dressed now too in a nightgown that almost certainly would be Amanda's. Either Amanda or LouAnne must have given her a wash and brushed her hair, because except for being pale, she appeared quite normal. For that matter, Longarm realized, she might have been pale to begin with.

He approached the bed. The woman looked up at him with no recognition whatsoever, so he said, "H'lo, miss. My name is Long. Custis Long. I'm a United States deputy marshal." He hesitated, then added, "It was my horse you tried to steal. I'm the one as shot you."

"Oh, I . . . I'm sorry, Marshal."

"Who are you, miss?"

"My name is Jane Nellis. Am I under arrest?"

"No. Not yet anyhow. Why were you tryin' to steal that horse, Miss Nellis?"

"It is Mrs. Nellis, not Miss. I . . . My husband. I think he has been murdered. And our daughter kidnapped."

Longarm's eyebrows went up. LouAnne reached out and took the woman's hand to offer comfort and encouragement.

"I was trying to go for help," Jane Nellis said. She was beginning to cry now. "Our daughter . . . she is only sixteen. The men took her. I can only imagine why."

"But you got away," Longarm said, not sure if the woman was telling the truth or merely angling for sympathy.

She nodded. "I slipped out under the back of the tent. I ran. Trying to get help. That is why . . . your horse . . . I'm sorry." The tears were coming heavy now, and snot streamed out of her nose.

"Tent?" he asked. "You were in a tent?"

"My husband . . . Frank Nellis . . . he is a geologist. We found . . . silver. Commer . . . commercial quantities . . . he thought. Was going to file . . . claim."

Longarm could see that Jane Nellis was tiring. Her complexion was looking gray and unhealthy.

"Who shot him, Mrs. Nellis? Who took your daughter?"

"I don't . . . Some men. I didn't know them. I think Frank did. Met them . . . I don't know."

"And this tent?" he asked. "Where is the tent that you say they raided?"

Her tears came even more heavily. "I don't . . . I don't *know*," she wailed. "Mountains. In the . . . mountains. I don't know where. Up . . . up there. Other side of mountain. I don't know."

"Custis. Please," Amanda said. "Can't you leave her alone now?" "And don't you worry," LouAnne put in. "The marshal will find those men. He will get your baby back for you."

Jane Nellis clutched LouAnne's hand. "Will he?"

"He will," LouAnne declared, nodding emphatically. "I promise he will."

That was news to Longarm, but Mrs. Nellis seemed to accept it as gospel. A smile flickered across her face. Then she closed her eyes and went back to sleep.

Longarm was not sure if he should thank LouAnne. Or punch the woman in the face.

Chapter 12

"Custis, we have to talk." Amanda was standing with her fists on her hips, looking like she was ready for a fight.

"'Bout what?" he asked.

"You know about what," Amanda returned.

LouAnne, looking more than a little uncomfortable, stood and said, "I'll put a pot of coffee on to boil." She quickly exited the parlor, where they had moved after Jane Nellis fell asleep.

"You have to find that little girl, Custis. You have to return her to her mother, and you have to find out what happened to her husband too. Why, the poor thing doesn't even know if she is a widow or not."

"She was coming here to report the crime to the local law. What's wrong with you going to find your local sheriff or somebody and letting him take care of it."

"Damn you, Custis, you know good and well that anything that happened on the other side of the mountain is outside the jurisdiction of our local people. They would just say it's a shame and go back home to bed. You, on the other hand, are a federal deputy. You have jurisdiction anywhere in the country."

"Kidnapping isn't a federal crime, Mandy," he reasoned.

"What about murder?" she countered.

"Murder neither. Not that we know for certain sure that anybody's been murdered."

"So . . . so . . . so maybe the kidnappers stole a piece of mail out of the Nellises' tent. I don't know, dammit. You figure it out. But in the meantime, go *do* something about it."

"I got to go back up there to get the stuff I cached up top," Longarm grumbled. "Maybe I could, um, maybe I could look around a mite. But there's an awful lot I'd need to know. Like how to find this silver strike that Frank Nellis is supposed to have made. Why, I don't even know the daughter's name."

"Sybil," LouAnne said from the doorway as she entered carrying a tray with a carafe and coffee cups.

"What?"

"The daughter. Her name is Sybil. I remember Jane saying that."

"I didn't hear any such," Longarm said.

"Before we came to get you," LouAnne said. She set the tray down and began pouring coffee and distributing a cup for each of them before finally pouring a cup for herself and settling onto the sofa. "She was talking about her little girl then. I remember she said the child's name is Sybil."

"What about the place where her husband made this silver find? Did she say anything about that?"

"Of course she did. Cream, Custis? Sugar?"

"No, thanks. What about the place?"

"She said it is in a canyon. There is a stream running through it. There aren't any roads. She didn't mention anything else."

"Hell, that covers pretty much half o' Colorado," Longarm said.

"Can't you trail her back to where she was?" Amanda asked.

Longarm grunted. "Track a woman afoot over rocky ground? I'm good, Mandy, but I'm no magician."

"Can't you even try?" LouAnne asked.

"Custis, you owe the lady that much."

"After all, Custis, you are the one who shot her."

"She might have gotten help sooner if you hadn't shot her."

"She would have given your horse back to you. She told me so."

"Whoa!" Longarm held a hand up, palm outward, to cut off the flow of comment and condemnation. "Hold up there, ladies. I've got to go up there anyway to get my stuff. Maybe, oh, maybe I'll take a quick look around while I'm there. See if I can find out anything about Nellis and the kid." He tried the coffee. It was getting cold already. Damn thin-walled china cups was the problem, he silently thought. A good, heavy mug will hold the heat where this thin porcelain crap will not.

And yes, dammit, he admitted to himself, he was putting off saying what he knew good and well he would have to say.

He sighed and said, "I'll look for the girl. All right?"

Both Amanda and LouAnne smiled broadly. LouAnne picked up the carafe and leaned forward. "Can I heat your coffee, dear?"

Chapter 13

Longarm stretched out on the sofa for the remainder of the night. When he woke up, he could hear the boarders coming downstairs for breakfast. His stomach rumbled a little at the thought of breakfast. He got up and went back into the kitchen.

He did not want to confuse the paying folks by showing up at the dining table for breakfast, but that did not stop him from grabbing a plate in the kitchen and helping himself to the platters of food before Amanda carried them into the dining room, and LouAnne made sure his coffee cup never became empty.

Two women waiting on him! That sounded mighty good as far as he was concerned.

After breakfast both women gave him passionate good-bye kisses. Each of them fingered his crotch and whispered promises in his ear.

"Now I'm damn sure anxious t' get back," he said.

"We'll play all you like then, Custis, but right now go. Go!" Amanda said.

"Hurry back, Custis. But go. Go!" LouAnne said.

"I could put this off for a day or two," he suggested, not entirely joking.

"Go!" both chorused as one voice.

He went. Went outside to collect his horse and burro. It took only a moment to throw the comfortable civilian saddle onto the brown mare and step onto her back, with the fuzzy-eared burro trailing at the end of the lead rope.

He had gotten a late start but this time was riding with intent rather than simply ambling along on vacation. It was still daylight—although barely—when he reached the barren patch of ground on top of the mountain where he had left his packs.

Some passing travelers had used the stack of firewood he had laid there, but his things were untouched. The unknown travelers were honest men, it seemed, and he wished them well.

Once again he laid his bedroll out on the rocky ground, and while he still had a little daylight he scrounged enough wood for coffee come morning.

Longarm sat for a time smoking and looking out over the wave after wave of mountain peaks laid out before him. Frank Nellis's silver lode could be hidden within any of the thousand canyons that lay north of Silver Plume.

And the kidnappers of a sixteen-year-old girl named Sybil could be in any of those canyons or in any of the countless villages and mining camps out there.

How in hell was he supposed to find either? he mused.

He was fretting about those questions when he lay down to sleep, but he was finding no answers to them.

Chapter 14

There were three men. No, correct that, there were at least three men. There could have been more, he supposed.

The number that he was reasonably sure of came from Jane Nellis by way of LouAnne, who said it was the way Jane described it to her in her rambling. Three men and one little girl. At least he sure as hell *hoped* there was still a girl out there to find. It was not beyond the realm of possibility that the sons of bitches took her, used her, and threw her away.

Despite his grumbling back there in Silver Plume, the thought of a child being abused made Longarm's blood boil.

He had no jurisdiction over most common crimes, up to and including murder. He could not go after these men in his capacity as a deputy United States marshal.

But as Custis Long, private citizen . . . the bastards would do well to go find a judge and throw themselves at his feet. Beg the man for protection inside a jail cell. Because the wrath of a thoroughly pissed off private citizen could be an awesome thing to behold.

It would be even worse to view from the muzzle end of Longarm's .45.

With any luck . . .

He stirred the coals of last night's fire and built it afresh, put a short pot of coffee on to boil, and took the rest of his water to the brown mare and the fuzzy burro. By the time he was done with them, his coffee water was bubbling at a brisk boil.

He used a stick to lift the lid off the pot and tossed in a handful of ready-ground coffee, then pawed through his saddlebags until he found a chunk of jerky that did not have too much lint sticking to it. That and the steaming hot—if a trifle weak—coffee was breakfast. Not quite in the same category as the plates and platters of biscuits, sausage, flapjacks, and gravy he'd had back in Amanda's kitchen, but it would do.

When he was done with his sketchy meal, he poured the leftover coffee back into his canteen and saddled the mare. The burro took his packs without complaint, and once again their little caravan took to the trail, this time winding ever lower on the north shoulder of the mountain that sheltered Silver Plume.

Three or more men and a little girl.

They could be anywhere.

He intended to find them.

Chapter 15

"No, sir, I don't recall any such," the gent leading the pack train said. He turned in his saddle and motioned for his helper to come up from the back of the train. "Say, Bob, you seen anything of a bunch of men, three or maybe more of 'em, traveling with a young girl? Would've been sometime in the past few days. This fella here is looking for 'em."

The helper rode around their string of mules and stopped beside the leader. He scratched his beard for a moment in thought, then shook his head. "Seen a couple other pack trains, but there wasn't no women with them. Sorry."

Longarm's fear was that a group with no females included might only mean that the girl was dead by now, but that was not something that would be easy to ascertain, certainly not just by looking. Hell, for all he knew these two could have been among the men who raided the Nellis camp and took the girl.

And what of Frank Nellis? If he were still alive, surely he would show up somewhere soon. Or languish and die somewhere in one of those countless canyons if he'd been wounded and left behind by the raiders.

Come to think of it, why did Jane Nellis abandon the man? Sheer terror, he supposed. Nighttime. Guns going off.

Her daughter in the hands of the raiders. So she ran. It was not an unreasonable thing to do.

Longarm had known women with sand, women who would have fought the raiders tooth and toenail to defend their child. Jane Nellis was not that kind.

She did run for help, she said. That was what brought her to his little mountaintop camp, trying to steal a horse.

Now the woman lay in Amanda Carricker's feather bed, warm and comfortable and well fed. Taken care of by a pair of helpful women while he was up here on the mountain trails trying to sort out what had happened to her daughter.

With very little effort, Longarm could resent Jane Nellis.

But then who was he to judge? Certainly he would have reacted differently in that situation. But he was not a frightened, perhaps normally timid woman under assault by strangers, strangers who shot her husband and may well have killed the man.

He sighed and thanked the men with this pack train. It was the third he had encountered and stopped to question so far today. No one had seen three or more men traveling with a young girl.

"Good luck to you, mister," one of them said, pulling his horse off the trail and motioning for his partner to lead their mule train on up the mountain.

"And to you," Longarm returned.

He nipped the twist off a cheroot, lighted the slender cigar, and hooked a knee over his saddle horn. He sat smoking—and thinking—while the mule train lumbered past on its way south to Silver Plume or beyond.

There were times, Longarm had to admit, when he wished he had the sort of simple life that those men had. Nothing to worry about except their animals and getting their cargo delivered on time.

He grinned and blew out a series of smoke rings. Who the hell was he kidding anyway? He had tried the simple life. He had cowboyed, worked half a dozen other jobs. None of them had challenged him the way this one did. He was proud of his deputy U.S. marshal's badge. He was proud of the work he did with it.

And now he would be proud—and damned lucky too—if he could find out what happened to Sybil Nellis and get the kid back to her mother.

The first step toward that end, he knew, would be to find Frank Nellis's prospecting camp. That had to be the starting point. Everything else would follow.

Longarm touched the brim of his Stetson in a silent salute of thanks to the tail man on the mule train, let the last animal pass, and then started on down the winding trail he had been following since morning.

Chapter 16

Shortly before sundown Longarm reached a . . . he supposed it would be considered a village. Certainly it was not a town, but it was larger and better established than a mere encampment. It remained to be seen whether it would survive and prosper enough to eventually become a town.

A sign carved into a split shingle and posted beside the road read BEDLAM.

Longarm did not know the cause for Bedlam being established here beside a rushing mountain stream. Almost certainly the people here would be mining something from the rock, silver or gold, copper or magnesium. What really mattered was whether there was enough of the material to justify the creation of a real town.

As it was, Bedlam was mostly a collection of tents. Half a dozen structures along the side of the main street had log walls and canvas roofs. Those, Longarm assumed, would be business locations. The population lived either in tents or in mud dugouts carved into the sides of the canyon.

Longarm located a cook tent mostly by following his nose. Literally. A mouthwatering scent of frying meat reached him even before he entered Bedlam, and he followed it to a ragged

tent where two men and a haggard woman were cooking slabs
of meat and a huge pot of rice.

The diners lined up under the shelter of a canvas fly, paid
their two bits, and walked away with a tin plate of meat and
rice. Split logs laid beside the creek served for seating. You
brought your own utensils if you wanted any—a good many
of the men who were having their supper now did without,
just grabbing with their hands and shoveling food in as best
they could—and you were expected to turn your plate in
when you were finished. Washing those plates appeared to
be optional, although perhaps the owners of the establish-
ment would do some washing up between meals.

Longarm tied his horse to a sapling that somehow had
survived the rush to collect wood, paid his quarter, and got
his plate.

"Beef?" he asked the man who slapped the slab of meat
onto his plate.

"You have to be kidding, mister. It's elk."

"Ah, right."

"That okay with you?"

"Plenty. Elk is perfect by me."

"Move along then. There's others that want to eat too."

Longarm was fairly sure that Colorado had enacted game
laws that restricted the taking of elk to the fall and winter,
and this meat was certainly fresh. And out of season.

Not that it was any of his business. Out of his jurisdiction, like so much of what he was running into lately.

He had a fork in his packs on the burro, but he did not
want to bother digging it out. He settled for a seat on one of
the log benches, picked up the chunk of fried elk steak and
gnawed a hunk off with his teeth. The meat was tasty. A
little dry but otherwise past excellent, the poorest elk being
better than any piece of beef he could get in the finest res-
taurant in Denver.

The rice, of course, presented a messier problem, but
hunger made up for the lack of that fork. He scooped the

fluffy grains onto his fingers and stuffed them into his mouth the way nearly everyone around him was. The rice had a slightly nutty flavor. It was not his favorite food, but out here it made sense. It was easy to transport in bulk, cooked up larger than when dry, and stored far easier than potatoes.

Longarm was nearly done with his supper when he saw someone standing on the other side of his burro.

Longarm dropped his plate unheeded onto the muddy ground and ran across what passed for a street.

A man in bib overalls and a tattered red undershirt had one hand stuffed into one of Longarm's packs while trying to appear disinterested, as if he just happened to be standing beside the burro.

Longarm did not wait for an explanation.

He charged the thieving son of a bitch and used that momentum behind a powerful right, straight to the thief's jaw.

The man went down, out cold or as close to it as did not matter.

Longarm barely stopped himself from delivering a kick once he had the piece of shit down on the ground.

He stepped back, ready to take on any of the man's friends who wanted to join in, but not only did no one come to the fellow's defense, no one seemed to pay any attention to the dustup.

The one reaction he did get was from one of the cooks in the dining tent. "Hey, you. Pick up that plate and put it in the bucket if you expect to eat here again."

Welcome to Bedlam, Longarm thought, as he went back to collect his plate and put it into the bucket ready for the next man.

Chapter 17

A gent who had shipped in some five-gallon casks of whiskey—or anyway of alcohol, since coloring and water could be added locally—was doing a bang-up business in a large tent beside the creek. Longarm stepped up to the raw plank that was serving as a bar and laid a quarter down.

"You want change or a second shot?" the barkeep asked. The man was tall and bald and seemed to have no joints in his floppy limbs.

"The shot," Longarm told him.

The fellow bared his teeth in a grin. "Ah, you're a brave man," he said as he poured a double shot into a mug. "I have water if you want to cut that."

"Thanks, but let me try it first." Longarm tasted the raw whiskey, made a sour face, and shivered. "Good Lord, man, what'd you put in this stuff?"

The grin flashed again. "You don't want to know."

"Friend, I believe you're right about that."

"So, do you want some water to smooth that out?"

"Did you dip it out of the creek over there?"

"Yeah. The fellows pissing upstream give it that snappy flavor."

Before Longarm could react, he added, "But I'm joshing

you about that. We have a well over there a ways." He pointed.
"I get my water from there. Although I would think that
whiskey would be strong enough to cleanse pretty much
anything it touched."

Longarm tried the vile stuff again. It went down easier
that time.

"Water?" the barman offered again.

Longarm shook his head and tossed back the rest of the
liquor. "Whew! One more time then." He placed another
quarter on the plank. It quickly disappeared, and another
double shot was poured into his mug.

"I'm looking for some folks," he said.

"One second, friend." The barman held up a finger,
turned, and hurried down to the other end of the plank to
serve some other gents, then quickly returned to Longarm.
"You were saying?"

"I said I'm looking for some people. Three men. Traveling with a young girl."

"What do they look like?"

Longarm shrugged. "I don't know. That's the thing, I
don't know what they look like. I was told to meet them.
Three men . . . more could've joined them by now . . . and
a young girl."

"That isn't much to go on," the barman said.

"You aren't telling me anything I don't already know."

"Is it important that you meet these people?"

Longarm nodded. "It sure is."

"When are you supposed to meet them?"

"A couple days ago, actually. Is that a problem?"

"Not for me, it isn't," the friendly barkeep said with
another toothy grin. "If you like, though, I can keep my eyes
open. I'll let you know if I see anybody that might be your
party." The man was careful to avoid asking anything that
might have been of a personal nature, anything that Longarm might have taken offense to.

"I'd appreciate it. Thanks."

Longarm had another couple whiskeys—they tasted better and better the more he had of them—and went back out to collect his animals.

He walked a hundred yards or so outside Bedlam and laid out a camp of sorts. He did not need to cook for himself this time, not even coffee, but he could certainly use some sleep.

Bedlam was as noisy as, well, bedlam, but he was pretty much beyond the distance where the noise might bother him, so he stretched out in his blankets with his .45 resting in his hand. Just in case.

Then he closed his eyes and went promptly to sleep.

Chapter 18

"Shit!" Longarm snapped up into a sitting position seconds after a bullet slammed into his bed, not missing his head by more than inches.

"Watch where you're shooting, asshole. There's somebody tryin' to sleep over here," he yelled.

His answer was another gunshot. This time the slug passed on the other side of his head with a loud crack.

The son of a bitch was shooting at him deliberately.

Longarm jumped to his feet and snapped off a shot of his own. In the darkness he had nothing to aim at except the muzzle flash of the other man's gun, so he sent a .45-caliber sizzler of his own in that direction and was rewarded with a yelp. Whether that sound was a matter of pain or of frustration he could not tell.

He dropped back onto his blankets to pull his boots on, and another gunshot came at him out of the darkness, and from a different location.

This one passed overhead by a good two or three feet. Apparently they had not seen him drop down.

Two shooters? Or one man quietly on the move. He could not know that.

Longarm stayed low and moved silently in the direction

of that last gunshot, Colt in hand, alert for motion within the shadows. His night vision had been disrupted by his own gunfire, but it was returning now.

He did not know how long he had been asleep. More to the point, he did not know how long the nightly drinking and rowdiness in Bedlam generally went on, but by now there were few lights and no noise coming from the village. He would have welcomed more light, actually. It would have made it easier for him to find the bastard or bastards who'd shot at him.

Longarm darted forward from shadow to shadow all the way down to the creek without finding anyone to shoot at and without being shot at again himself.

Disgusted, he turned back uphill and returned to his bedroll.

It was quite obvious that whoever it was that wanted him dead knew where he had laid out his blankets. Equally obvious was that the person or persons, whoever he was or they were and whatever his or their motives were, could choose to try it again.

It just did not seem like much of a good idea to lie down and go back to sleep in that same spot, and so, reluctant but resigned to the necessity, Longarm saddled the mare and loaded his burro again. Then he led the two animals well away from Bedlam, to a grassy spot just above a grove of young aspen.

For the second time that night, Longarm laid out his bedding, removed his boots, and lay down.

This time he did not drop into sleep immediately. This time he lay awake for a little while trying to work out who might have wanted to shoot him.

Jane Nellis's attackers? They would certainly have good reason to want him dead or at least wounded badly enough to stop him from following them. But that made no sense. Not at this point, since they would have no way to know that Longarm existed, much less that he was on their trail.

He had seen no one in Bedlam he had ever encountered before. No wanted criminals who could have recognized him and assumed that he wanted them.

Of course just because he had seen no one like that, it was always possible that some wanted felon could have seen him and made the assumption.

Longarm sighed. This was some damn vacation he was having. He would have to remember to thank Billy Vail when he got back to Denver. Hell, working would be a relief after this vacation.

With that thought in mind, he drifted back into a light and fitful sleep.

Chapter 19

No one shot at him when he led his animals around the stand of aspen and down toward Bedlam. Longarm considered that to be something of a plus.

He walked into the town and back to that same cook tent.

"Twenty-five cents, mister. Cash only, no credit." It was the friendliest greeting—and the only one—he'd gotten that morning. He paid the quarter and plucked a tin plate out of the washtub beside the money man.

This time he had remembered to bring his own knife, fork, and spoon out of his pack.

Breakfast turned out to be flapjacks, all you wanted, with a ladle of sorghum syrup poured over them. He had had worse.

Longarm hunkered down and placed his plate on his knees, then proceeded to fill up. The hotcakes were thin but tasty, but the syrup had too much of a sulfur flavor for his taste. All in all, not bad.

After he finished gorging himself, he walked down beside the creek and had a smoke.

He was just walking back up toward his animals, wondering if he could find Frank Nellis's camp—and for that matter if he might find Frank Nellis—when it happened again.

Some sorry son of a bitch threw a shot at him.

He caught a glimpse of rapid movement off to his right. Looked that way and saw the familiar figure of the thief in the bib overalls and red undershirt.

This time the man had a rifle in his hands and was taking aim. At Longarm.

Chapter 20

Longarm did not really want to kill the man, despite the asshole's habit of shooting at people he did not like.

Longarm snapped off two shots, one beside each of the fellow's ears. The idea was to discourage him.

It did. Sort of.

At least it made him turn tail and run. But the idiot kept shooting; he stopped every few yards to turn and fire back at Longarm.

Fortunately he was a dreadfully bad shot. His bullets came fairly close, but they did not connect.

Longarm's worry was that if the thief kept this up, sooner or later he would get lucky. At which point Custis Long would be terribly *un*lucky. Sooner or later one of those slugs was going to hit, hit either Longarm or somebody else. Either of those would be bad. Longarm certainly did not want some bystander to be hit any more than he wanted to take a slug himself.

The only real defense he had, Longarm figured, was to properly discourage the son of a bitch.

He fired again, coming close to the man but careful to avoid hitting him.

The man must have heard the whip-crack of Longarm's

bullet sizzling past his ear, because he turned and ran. Ran
across the flimsy wooden bridge to the other side of the creek
and up the side of the hill on the far side. He disappeared
into the dark mouth of a mine opening after first tossing his
rifle aside.

Longarm followed, stopping every once in a while to
encourage the retreat by sending another .45 slug close to
his heels.

At the entrance to the dark and narrow mine, Longarm
was stopped by a burly fellow in overalls. The man had a
clipboard and an official air about him. He grabbed Longarm by the arm and yanked him to a stop.

"Are you after Henry?" he asked.

"I'm after the fella that just ran in here. I got no idea what
his name is."

"His name is Henry. You could say he's our town bully."

"And you could say," Longarm said, "that Henry is about
to get his ass whipped."

"That's fine," the miner said, "but you aren't going in
there with that pistol you're carrying."

"And why the hell not?" Longarm demanded.

"Because those cartridges are explosives, and explosives
cause concussion, and concussion like that can start a
cave-in. There's four men in there . . . no make that five if
you want to count Henry . . . that I'd just as soon *not* see die
in a damn cave-in. And that's to say nothing of the month or
so it might take to dig it all back out again. So bottom line
is, if you want to go in after Henry, be my guest. But you
aren't taking that gun in there with you."

Longarm frowned. But he removed his gunbelt and laid
it beside Henry's rifle. "Satisfied?" he asked.

"Yup," the miner said. "Oh, one more thing. You don't
know this place. You might want to take one of those carbide lamps." He grunted. "That's if you want to see past the
end of your nose once you get more than a few paces in."

There was a pile of the small but amazingly powerful

little lamps inside a shack beside the mine entrance. They were worn on the head like caps. The miners generally strapped them around soft caps. Longarm picked one up and examined the thing.

"Here, let me light it for you," the helpful fellow—Longarm assumed he was the foreman—said, taking the lamp and striking a match.

In broad daylight the lamp seemed to give off no light at all, but Longarm knew that once he was in darkness he would appreciate the bright glow. "Thanks, mister."

"Mind a piece of advice?"

"As long as I don't have t' promise to take it."

"Our Henry is a brawler. Nobody likes him, but nobody can whip him either. If you find him, take him fast and take him dirty, because that's what he'll try to do with you. Here." The fellow bent down and picked up a chunk of wood that was about three inches thick and three feet long. "If you can find him, use this."

Longarm whistled. "You boys play rough, don't you?"

"Neighbor, our Henry won't be playing. If you go in there, he'll try and kill you."

"He's been doing that already, damn him," Longarm snapped. "I'm tired of it. It stops here."

"Good luck to you then." The foreman stepped back and touched the brim of his soft cap.

Longarm took a deep breath. And entered the world of the miners.

Chapter 21

The adit—it was not a tunnel; tunnels go all the way through something—was roughly square in shape, four-and-a-half feet tall and approximately four feet wide. Longarm had to crouch to pass through.

He crabbed his way forward. After fifty feet or so the light from the adit mouth disappeared and he had to rely on the headlamp to see his way. The beauty of the simple lamp was that it pointed wherever he looked, allowing him to see another twenty or thirty feet ahead. If he turned his head to the side, the light turned with him.

The bent-over posture he was required to adopt was hard to maintain. He discovered that every few minutes he had to stop and hunker down on his heels in order to rest his thigh muscles. Then, refreshed, he could go on again, using the chunk of pine like a cane to ease a little of the strain on his back.

The adit had walls, ceiling, and floor of roughhewn rock, chipped painfully out of the live rock by men with chisels and hammers. Longarm could scarcely imagine the effort that had been required to complete that work for hundreds, perhaps for thousands of feet into the mountain. It had all been done, of course, to follow a vein of valuable ore of some mineral or metal.

He still did not know what they were mining here. Probably silver, but it could have been for any number of other minerals instead.

Right now his chore was to mine one asshole named Henry, who was hiding somewhere underground. One murderous asshole, he reminded himself. The man had already tried several times to kill him. It was a habit Longarm wanted to break him of.

The adit twisted left and right, up and down. Curiously, the floor was soft underfoot. He did not take time to examine the layer of brown padding spread on the floor.

Then the answer to what it was came to him. Came in the form of a string of burros plodding toward him out of the darkness, each of the eight small, shaggy animals carrying bulging packsaddles of raw ore.

That, he realized, explained the height of the opening. It was just high enough to accommodate a burro and just wide enough to accept the burro plus the width of the ore sacks it carried.

The intelligent little animals were making their journey with no human hand guiding them. Obviously they knew where they were going. Longarm had to drop down to hands and knees and press himself hard against the cold, stone wall at his side in order to let the string of burros pass.

He reached an opening to his left which turned out to be a larger, taller expanse where a large pocket of ore had been removed. The light from his lamp showed nothing but stone walls and on this floor rock chips instead of the burro manure that carpeted the main line.

There was no sign of Henry or of any other humans. Back in the main line he traveled perhaps another hundred yards before he encountered lights and voices. He came upon a group of four miners, each wearing a headlamp, with a collection of hammers, chisels, and pry bars at their sides.

"You lookin' for Henry?" asked one of the men, with such a grimy, rock-dust–covered face that Longarm was sure he would not recognize the fellow after he washed.

Longarm nodded, causing shadows to dance in front of him. "I am."

The man eyed the chunk of wood in Longarm's hand, then pursed his lips to point with. "About fifty feet in there's a branch to the left. Take it."

"Thanks." Longarm touched a finger to his forehead and moved past the men, who were taking a break with sandwiches and bottles of coffee.

He moved slowly in until he came to the side opening the miner had mentioned. The adit branched straight left and sloped upward to the right.

Longarm paused there.

Left, the man had said.

Too easily? Henry, after all, was one of their own. And Longarm was a stranger.

Longarm knelt for a moment to ease aching muscles not accustomed to this cramped posture.

Then he moved forward. Into the right-hand adit.

Chapter 22

If the would-be assassin was in there, he was sitting there with no headlamp marking his position. But then he knew this mine. And he did *not* want to be found.

Henry was the sort who preferred to murder without exposing himself to danger. That, Longarm thought, was the hallmark of a coward. Low, cunning, and sneaky. But cowardly. That seemed to describe Henry to the proverbial T.

There was no point in trying to be silent, Longarm realized. Not with his headlamp throwing a cone of light twenty feet in front of him. The bastard would be able to see him coming a hundred feet away.

He bent low but craned his neck to throw the light as flat and as far as possible. If he gave in to the fatigue of the bent-forward position and allowed his head to drop, that threw the light from his lamp onto the floor, practically at his feet, doing nothing at all to help him search for danger lying ahead.

Every few feet he had to stop, drop down onto his heels, and peer around as best he could.

Henry was somewhere ahead. He was sure of it. Well, fairly sure. He could have been wrong back there. The miner taking his lunch break could have been telling the truth about which way Henry went.

Longarm did not believe that. But then he had been wrong about things before now. He could well be wrong again here. If he were, that would allow Henry to get behind him, perhaps to flee from the mine while Longarm was still busy looking for him inside.

It was a risk. All Longarm could do was to use his best judgment and go on. And right now his best judgment was that his quarry was somewhere close ahead, waiting there to kill him with his bare hands.

Longarm spotted a shard of rock on the floor. It was long and thin, roughly the size and shape of a spike. Or a dagger.

He lay the piece of wood down and picked up the sliver of stone.

It occurred to him—too late—that he should have counted the number of hammers back there where the workmen were resting. Two teams of cutters? Probably. So there should have been two hammers in addition to two chisels. He had passed right on by without paying attention to the tools the men had with them that he might have made use of. A fatal mistake? It could have been.

There was no time to worry about that now. He had the stone knife. Henry might have . . . almost anything. Anything other than a firearm, that is.

Longarm craned his neck to look at the ceiling. It seemed solid to him, but the miners knew their trade far better than he ever would. If they said the rock was rotten and could come crashing down with the concussion from a gunshot, he was inclined to believe them.

Henry would know that too and would not risk death in a cave-in by trying to sneak a gun past the others.

When he attacked—if Longarm could find him—the man would come with anything at hand, rocks or knives or clubs . . . anything.

The adit Longarm was in opened up into a chamber where a large amount of ore had been removed from a concentrated area. He was able to almost, not quite but almost, stand erect in it. The change was a relief to his aching back.

He stood there for a moment, back arched, his lamp playing a cone of yellow light onto the ceiling.

He heard something. A faint skittering on the rock floor.

He looked down again—barely in time to see the big thief from the day before charging for his throat.

The man held a chunk of rock in his fist.

A rock bludgeon against a stone knife. Their combat had come down to Stone Age weapons in a modern-age fight to the death.

Longarm braced himself for the onslaught and involuntarily let out a low-pitched war cry as his enemy closed with him.

Chapter 23

The fight was swift and brutal, over in almost an instant. The big man swung his heavy rock at Longarm's head, intending to crush Longarm's skull with one hard swing.

Instead of pulling back, which Henry anticipated, Longarm drove forward, dropping underneath that roundhouse swing and jabbing Henry in the gut with his sharp, pointed shard of stone.

The stone knife was wrenched out of his hand when Henry turned, grunting loudly.

Longarm was so close that he could smell garlic heavy on the big man's breath.

When Henry pulled his bludgeon back, he grazed Longarm's ear and knocked Longarm's head lamp completely off, sending the carbide lamp tumbling to the floor, where it gave off a ghostly light.

Longarm grappled with the bastard.

Henry's hands groped for Longarm's throat, but Longarm clenched his hands together and drove them upward, knocking Henry's hands away.

Longarm pummeled Henry in the face and throat, drawing blood and a roar of rage.

Henry succeeded in grasping Longarm by the throat. He

squeezed. Longarm could feel his consciousness fading. His vision turned red and blurred.

He knew if he did not break the hold soon he would die. He managed to get a grip on Henry's little finger. He pulled. Hard. He heard the distinctive crack of a bone breaking, and Henry let out another roar.

More to the point, his grip on Longarm's throat loosened a little.

Longarm shifted his grip from the broken finger to Henry's wrist. He twisted and pulled, ripping that hand away from his throat so he could grab the other wrist with both hands. He twisted, forcing Henry's hand away from his throat and down.

Longarm elbowed the man in the face. He felt cartilage snap. Felt the hot rush of blood flooding over him.

Henry cried out again but not so strongly this time. The big man seemed to weaken. He sagged to his knees, coming down almost on top of Longarm's headlamp.

Longarm stepped back, his breathing heavy after those few seconds of mortal combat.

The glare of light from the carbide lamp showed Henry slumped on his side. The stone knife Longarm had been carrying was buried half its length into his gut, high under his ribs. The man must have been bleeding internally ever since that first clash of bodies.

Henry gasped for air, mouth forming an O like a fish tossed onto a riverbank. One hand lifted as if in surrender.

It was no surrender. He tried in vain to punch Longarm but no longer had strength enough to throw the fist. His hand fell helpless across his body.

His mouth opened and for a moment Longarm thought he wanted to speak. Instead a gout of blood, dark in the light from the fallen headlamp, spilled out of his mouth to saturate his beard and dribble down onto the rock floor.

He clearly was dying.

Longarm rocked back onto his heels, gasping for breath himself. He shook his head.

"A waste," he said, his voice coming out halfway between a croak and a whisper. "What a stupid, fucking waste."

Longarm dropped down, sitting with his back pressed against the rock wall. He picked up the headlamp and put it on, then sat with the man called Henry until the man's breathing stopped and his eyes glazed into the blank sightlessness of death.

When Longarm's breathing had returned to normal, he knelt and closed Henry's eyes, then started back out toward the mine entrance.

He encountered the four workmen on his way out, the patient little burros following close behind them.

"Your buddy is back there," he told the men. "You can haul his ass out; I'm not gonna do it for you."

All four blinked, uncomprehending.

Longarm crouched low until the last burro was past, then resumed his low duckwalk back to sunlight and fresh air.

Chapter 24

Her husband had made a find of some sort, Jane Nellis had said. Presumably then the three raiders wanted his claim as much as, or more than, whatever they might have been able to rob from the site.

Well, they wanted the claim and wanted the girl as well.

The problem was that Jane Nellis had no idea where her husband's find was located. She had been there, of course, but did not know where she was at the time.

Jane was a city girl with no knowledge of these mountains. Her only interest was with her family, her only reason for being there was to be with them.

And now her family was gone. Somewhere in these mountains, in one of the innumerable gulches and valleys. Even if Jane had been willing to go back, even if she were sufficiently recovered from her ordeal . . . and from the gunshot wound Longarm put into her . . . she would not know how to find her way back.

Longarm knew he could wander these mountains for the next couple years and might or might not find his way into the right gulch. Worse, if he did find it, he might well not know it was the right place. Any new diggings with three or more owners? Wouldn't that be a futile telltale to look for since parties of miners often banded together to find and work their claims.

The only thing he could think of was how the mind of the average criminal worked.

The bastards could not themselves be trusted, and so they tended to not trust others. Apparently they assumed that everyone was as crooked as they were themselves.

When he reached the opening of the adit where Henry died, Longarm retrieved his .45 and said to the foreman there, "Mind if I ask you something?"

"Don't mind at all. So what's your question?"

"Up here, when a man makes a strike, where does he go to file his claim?"

The foreman turned his head and spat a stream of pale tobacco juice off to the side, then turned his attention back to Longarm. "You gotta post your markers at each of the four corners, then you go all the way down to Fort Collins. There's a government office where you fill out the forms and pay a five-dollar filing fee. But just in case you're wondering, this outfit is properly filed on, everything nice and legal."

"Thanks," Longarm said.

"Now do you mind if I ask you something?" the foreman asked.

"Not at all. What d'you want to know?"

"That son of a bitch Henry. Did you find him?"

Longarm nodded. "I found him."

"But you're still upright and breathing."

"Yes, but I'm afraid he isn't. They'll be bringing him out directly, I'd reckon."

"Fast and dirty?" the foreman asked.

"He tried."

"You're lucky."

"That I am," Longarm agreed, reaching for a cheroot. When he struck a match to light it, he discovered that his hand was shaking.

What he needed, he decided, was a drink. Or two.

Fortunately, Bedlam was well equipped to supply that need.

"Thanks for your help," he said, touching the brim of his Stetson to the foreman.

Then, stiff and sore but still alive, he walked down to the creek and across to the business side of things, where there was whiskey available to ease a man's ills.

Chapter 25

Longarm had his drink and then another. Finally he summoned the barkeep over to him. The man reached for a jug to pour from, but Longarm stopped him.

"I'm needin' information," he said, "and I'm hoping you can tell me."

"Depends," the bartender said. "What is it you're wanting to know?"

"What's the best way to get down to Fort Collins?" Longarm asked.

The barman turned and pointed. "See that road out there?"

"Sure," Longarm said.

"Follow it. All you got to do is go downhill. When you get out of the mountains, look around. You'll be in Fort Collins." The man picked up the whiskey jug. "Do you want another or not?"

Longarm nodded. "One more, then I reckon I'd best be on my way." He had that one, thanked the bartender, and made his way back to his mare and burro.

Fort Collins, or more to the point the nearest mining claims office, was a day and a half away. Longarm camped on the banks of the Cache la Poudre for the night and made it on into the town past noon the following day.

He was tired, all the more so because he doubted that he would learn anything here that would help him find the three men who had kidnapped Sybil Nellis and sent Jane Nellis into a panic.

Still, if you have only one card to play . . . play it.

He got directions to the government land office, and then, assured that he knew where he was going, he found the nearest café. He had not had lunch and was hungry as well as weary.

He tied the mare and the burro to a hitch ring on the side of the street, stretched, and paused for a yawn, then went inside. Immediately he was surrounded with the scents of freshly baked pies and roasted meats. They made his mouth water.

Longarm was the only customer in the place, it being too late for lunch and too early for supper. His entry was announced by a small bell hanging in the doorway, where the opening or closing of the door would ring it.

The ring was answered by a plump woman with her hair piled into a bun. She was red-faced and sweating and appeared none too pleased to see him. She emerged from a back room wearing an apron and a scowl. "Who are you?" she demanded.

"I, uh, I just came in for somethin' to eat. If you ain't open or, um, or something, just say so."

She gave him a suspicious glare and said, "You aren't one of McGuire's men?"

"I'm a man. I'll go that far with it, but I don't know anybody named McGuire. Look, if you want me t' go someplace else, just say so. I don't wanna be a bother to you."

"No, I . . . Never mind." She plucked a towel off the counter nearby and wiped her hands with it. "What can I get you?"

Chapter 26

The pot roast and red-jacket potatoes were as good as they smelled, and the meal included seconds. Or, in Longarm's case, thirds.

He broke a soft roll in half and was using it to sop up the gravy on his plate when the waitress/cook/dishwasher/owner stopped in front of him and placed a small plate down. It held what appeared to be rhubarb pie, the pastry crust sparkling with baked on white sugar.

"Got room?" she asked with a smile.

"If that's as good as it looks, I'll make room," he answered.

Longarm pulled the plate toward him and picked up his fork.

Behind him the door bell tinkled, and two men came in. Longarm glanced over his shoulder, then returned his attention to the rhubarb pie. His fork was poised over that tasty-looking crust when one of the gents at the door said, "Get out."

Longarm half turned again. "Are you talkin' to me?"

"That's right," the man in the lead growled. "Out." He hooked a thumb over his shoulder to point the way to the door and the street beyond. "No one's eating here."

Longarm laid his fork down and swung around on the counter stool so he could face the two.

Both of the men were dressed in town clothes, more like workingmen than clerks. They wore heavy shoes, overalls, and knit caps. And they looked angry for some reason.

"Get out," the second one repeated.

Longarm frowned. "I haven't finished my meal."

"You've finished, cowboy. Now, get the fuck out of here."

Longarm smiled at them. "Two things," he said. "First off, you shouldn't use language like that in front of a lady. And second, I already told you, I ain't finished eating." The smile disappeared, replaced by a glacial stare. "Now, fuck off before I get mad an' leave this here stool. And you don't want that. Trust me, boys, you don't."

The nearer man, a lanky fellow with a close-trimmed beard and a mouse under his left eye, grinned at that. He turned to his friend and said, "I think the pilgrim here wants to get his ass whipped, Tommy me lad." To Longarm he said, "Mister, you can either get up and leave nice and quiet, or you can stay where you are and we'll throw your ass out. Your choice."

"You know the choice I'm making, boys." Longarm was peeved to begin with, his vacation having been ruined, to say nothing of the fate of little Sybil Nellis. He flew off the stool, charging straight at them.

Before the nearer man had time to mount a defense, Longarm's hard right fist turned his nose into red pulp, blood flowing into his beard. He staggered backward, flailing his arms in an attempt to keep his balance. He failed. He went down onto his butt.

By that time Longarm was onto the man called Tommy. Tommy had more time to prepare himself for this irate stranger. He put up his fists to block Longarm's right, only to be tattooed by a left hook followed by an uppercut into his breadbasket.

Tommy turned pale, doubled over with a groan, and tottered a few paces away.

Longarm turned back in time to see the man with the nosebleed come off the floor with fire in his eye.

That did not last very long.

He rose up just in time to take another hard right to his already damaged nose.

Blood flew onto the nearby tables and he went down again, this time taking a pair of chairs crashing to the floor with him.

Tommy was down as well, lying on his side and retching like he was about to puke up everything he had eaten in the past week.

"Well?" Longarm demanded, standing over them with his fists balled and his blood up. "Get up, damn you. Get up and try me again."

Instead Nosebleed staggered to his feet with the assistance of a table to cling to. He bent over Tommy and grabbed him by the elbow. "C'mon, lad. I don't think we're wanted here. Let's go."

Longarm waited until the two were out of the door, then he returned to his stool and that rhubarb pie.

Chapter 27

Longarm finished the pie—it was every bit as good as it looked—stood, and dug a hand into his pocket.

"No you don't," the plump cook said.

"Pardon?"

"Don't be bringing out any money. You don't owe me a thing."

"Ma'am, I like to eat you outa enough t' feed five lumberjacks. Surely I should pay for all that," he objected.

"Mister, it was worth that and twice as much again to see those two shakedown artists crawl out of here."

"Shakedown, eh? That's not good," Longarm said. "I just hope I haven't caused a problem for you once I'm out of here."

The woman shrugged. "No more of a problem than I would have if you hadn't whipped their butts and thrown them out. Anyway, I enjoyed seeing it. You made my day."

"But they can come back," he said, "and it could go hard on you."

"I'll cross that bridge when I come to it."

Longarm smiled. "You're a gutsy lady. I got t' say that for you."

"Not really. But I will admit that I can out-stubborn a

Missouri mule. Listen, can I get you anything else? Anything at all?"

She seemed anxious that he not leave the café just yet. Worried about those men returning, he supposed.

Longarm had work to do. Well, sort of. He needed to go over to that land claim office and see if he could get an idea of whether a claim had been filed in the past few days. And where.

On the other hand he did not want to take this lady's food and then toss her to the wolves. He was afraid that once he left the place, those shakedown boys would be back. Afraid that it might go hard on the woman if—when—that happened.

"Look, have you talked to the police about this? The local sheriff? Anybody?" he asked.

"Oh, I tried that. The first time they came in here, they demanded money. When I refused to pay, they broke up some things and threw all the food I had cooked out into the street. I locked up and went straight to our police chief." She scowled. "You see what good that did. The police took down a report. On my way out the door I glanced back toward the chief. I saw him wad the report up and toss it into the trash. I don't actually know anything, of course, but I suspect that Tim McGuire is paying the chief to look the other way."

"McGuire? Was he one of the ones who was just in here?" Longarm asked.

"Oh, no. McGuire doesn't soil his hands on the likes of me. He has employees who do that sort of thing. Employees who do all manner of other things too." She sniffed her disapproval.

"Ladies of the night?" Longarm guessed.

"Exactly. The man is a whoremonger and a scoundrel. And I do not use that ugly word lightly."

Longarm grunted. Then he smiled and said, "Thank you for the meal. It was excellent."

"Come anytime. You will always be welcome here."

"Thanks. But only if you promise to let me pay for my supper next time."

"That is a promise," she said, wiping her hands on her apron and reaching for a broom.

Longarm went out onto the sidewalk and stood for a moment, wondering which way he should turn now.

Chapter 28

He got directions, then walked past the land office and on to a building three blocks away.

The office he wanted was on the third floor. The receptionist was large and hairy and looked more like a bodyguard than an office worker.

"Mr. McGuire, please."

"I don't know you," the bodyguard said. The man needed a shave, Longarm thought. Needed to buy a better shoulder holster too; this one showed itself too much.

Longarm smiled, innocent as a newborn baby. "That's right, you don't. Mr. McGuire, please."

"You don't have an appointment," Ugly said.

"No, I don't. Mr. McGuire, please." Longarm's .45 came out and found its way to a point just beneath Ugly's nose. "Now!" He reached down and lifted the snub-nosed revolver out of the shoulder holster.

Longarm stepped back, and the bodyguard, a little pale now, stood and went to a door at the back of the room. He opened it and leaned inside. "There is, um, there is a man here to see you, Boss. He, uh, he didn't give a name."

"I don't want to see nobody, Jimmy. Tell the fucker to go away."

Longarm stepped inside behind Jimmy and shut the door in the big man's face. "This fucker don't feel like going away, Tim," he said. His smile returned, and he nodded to the fellows who were standing in front of their boss's desk. "Nice t' see you boys again. Now get out o' here while I talk to Mr. McGuire."

The two shakedown goons looked at their boss, who nodded. They immediately filed out, leaving Longarm alone with McGuire.

Big Tim McGuire had the look of a street fighter who had made his way up in the world. His suit was handsomely tailored. His cravat was perfectly tied, and a diamond stickpin the size of a quail egg—or a very good imitation of one—nested on the knot. His feet were propped up on his desk, displaying yellow spats and patent leather shoes. He wore the trappings of a gentleman, but his very often pulped nose and the puffiness around his eyes said he was a brawler at heart and always had been.

McGuire dropped his feet to the floor and swiveled his chair around to face Longarm. "Who the hell are you?"

"I'm the fellow who is gonna blow your sorry ass to kingdom come if you fuck with my friend anymore," Longarm told him.

"Your friend? Who the hell would that be?"

"The lady that runs Belina's Café over on Fourth. Your inept bullyboys were just over there trying to shake her down. I expect that's what they were in here to tell you. That I run them out o' the place. Next time I wouldn't go so easy on them. And if there is a next time, it'd go hard on you too. I'd find you, Tim. Find you and put a .45-caliber sizzler up your left nostril. Blow your empty brains right out o' your head. Am I making myself clear?"

"I got protection, you know," McGuire said.

"Not from me, you don't," Longarm told him, stroking the butt of his Colt while he did so. "An' not from my boys if anything was to happen to me."

"Your, uh, boys?"

"Federal deputies. They wouldn't be scared off by any o' your paid-off locals. They'd put you away, either by hanging or life inside. Their choice, not yours."

"Why the hell would a federal deputy give a shit about you, mister?"

Longarm grinned. And flipped his wallet open, showing his badge. "Now d'you understand?"

McGuire swallowed and leaned forward. "Belina's, you said?"

Longarm nodded. "The lady is a friend. It'd distress me if I was to ever hear she was bothered again. So drop her off your list, and I'll drop you off mine. It seems a fair trade-off to me. How does it strike you?"

"I, uh, sure, Marshal. I'll be leaving her alone from now on."

"Then we have no quarrel between us, Tim." Longarm touched the brim of his hat and nodded. "Have yourself a nice day."

He turned toward the door to leave. Heard McGuire's chair springs squeak. Spun around in time to see Big Tim McGuire reach into a desk drawer and bring out a Webley .455 revolver.

McGuire might have been good with his fists. But he was not nearly as quick with a gun as Longarm.

It was the last mistake he would ever make.

Chapter 29

Caught in the act of rising, the Webley in hand, McGuire was slammed back into his chair by the impact of Longarm's .45 slugs. The first took him in the belly. A second bullet tore his throat out.

"Oh, shit," Longarm mumbled, glancing quickly around. There was no other door, and at least three of McGuire's men were in that outer office.

He snatched out from behind his belt the revolver he had taken from the bodyguard, and looked at it. The snub-nose was small and compact, but it was a mean little thing, .38 caliber and fully loaded with six rounds.

Longarm stepped around behind McGuire's desk and appropriated his .455 caliber to go with the other two guns. If all three of them charged the office he wanted all the firepower he could manage.

And if he had to shoot his way out of this office, he wanted firepower more than ever. A shotgun loaded with buckshot would have been nice.

He just hoped those men out there did not have any shotguns close to hand themselves.

Longarm pushed his own Colt into its leather and knelt beside Big Tim McGuire's lifeless corpse. He did not have

long to wait. The door was flung open and the bodyguard
came rushing in.

Longarm drilled the man in the chest with the .455. The
bodyguard stopped, looked down at the hole in his shirt . . .
and toppled face forward onto the floor. Longarm only then
noticed that the man's hands were empty. He had been coming to his boss's assistance, but with his fists rather than
a gun.

One down and . . .

No one else charged the smoke-filled room. Longarm
waited a minute or so, then carefully—*very* carefully—
approached the doorway.

The outer office was empty. The two shakedown boys
had gone.

He was halfway down the stairs when a herd of local
cops wearing their blue and brass came rushing in. The two
goons were close behind them.

Chapter 30

"That's him, Bobby. That's the son of a bitch. Him and Big Tim was in the office alone. We heard shooting. Now he's standing here and Tim . . . where is Big Tim, eh? I ask you that. Where is the boss if he's here not even hurt a little bit?"

"Put your hands high, mister. Don't even think about reaching for one of those guns you're carrying," the cop in the lead shouted. "Touch a gun and we'll all drill you."

Which would have been a spectacular feat, Longarm thought, since the cops were carrying batons, but not a one of them had a firearm in his hands.

Still, he did the sensible thing. He raised his hands. After all, he did not have any desire to shoot down half the local police population. More importantly, he did not want to be shot down by them if or when they got around to dragging iron.

"Go easy, boys. I was just defending myself," he shouted. "There's no need for anybody to get testy here."

The cops came swarming up the stairs. The one in the lead snatched the pistols from him, his own Colt plus the .455 and the .38 that he still had stuffed behind his belt.

"Turn around, damn you," the cop shouted.

Longarm turned around.

"Hands behind you, mister."

He felt the steel of the handcuffs that the policeman snapped around his wrists. And none too gently either.

"Can I tell you . . . ," Longarm began, only to be cut short by a curt "Shut the fuck up" and a jerk on the handcuffs. So he shut the fuck up.

The lead cop shoved him over to the side of the staircase while the rest of the herd thundered past on their way up to the landing and into Big Tim McGuire's offices.

That inspection took only a moment before one of them rushed back with the news. "They're dead, Bobby. Everybody in there is dead. There's blood all over the damn place. That son of a bitch murdered them."

"You bastard!" Bobby snarled. The cop tried to smash his nightstick into the small of Longarm's back, aiming for the kidneys, but Longarm's chained wrists got in the way.

Even so, the pain drove Longarm to his knees, and he worried that perhaps his right wrist had been broken.

"Son of a bitch," the cop barked and struck with the nightstick again.

Longarm considered turning around and knocking the dumb bastard down the flight of stairs. With luck he would break his miserable neck.

But that would only make matters worse, dammit. Very reluctantly he held his tongue. But it was not easy.

More of the cops came down the stairs. They grabbed Longarm by the arms, turned him around, and hustled him down to the ground floor. They were not very gentle about it, but at least they did not push him down the stairs. He supposed he should be grateful for that.

"Outside," one of them ordered. Not that he had any choice about complying. The bunch of them duckwalked him out the door.

A Black Maria was just pulling up to the front of the building with more cops in it. They must have the entire police force on hand, Longarm thought.

The driver's helper jumped down and opened wide the doors at the back of the prisoner wagon.

"Get in," a voice behind him snapped.

The police very helpfully assisted him in climbing into the Maria. They were so very helpful that he hit the floor hard and skidded all the way to the front of the wagon, the breath knocked out of him and perhaps some bruises added to the others he'd recently collected.

The doors slammed shut. He heard the rattle of locks and then felt the wagon box sway as the helper climbed back onto the driving seat. He heard the driver call to his team. Felt the outfit lurch into motion.

Longarm did not know where they were going, but he hoped it was someplace reasonably within the public view and not to some convenient killing ground. Such things were not entirely unheard of. He could handle a beating if he had to. After all, he was no virgin when it came to such. But a bullet in the back of the head would be a little harder to deal with.

"Whoa," he heard the driver call after a very short journey on the streets of Fort Collins.

Then the doors were flung open and Custis Long was dragged bodily out of the Maria.

Chapter 31

Longarm woke up. He wished he hadn't.

If there was a place on his body that did not hurt, he could not identify it.

He had been kicked and pummeled and thoroughly beaten. He had been hit with nightsticks, fists, and boots. His balls ached, and his eyes were swollen closed to mere slits. Hell, his hair hurt! It had been, he had to admit, a first-class beating.

The good thing was that he had not been there for much of it. Repeated blows to the head had put his lights out fairly early in the game.

Now he wished he could fall unconscious again until, say, next Thursday or so. Jesus, he hurt.

He heard a grinding of metal on metal and the clang of a cell door being opened.

"All right, you. Out," a voice growled.

Longarm lay still. Actually he was not sure he *could* move, was not sure if important parts had been broken by the beating.

He tried to open his eyes, but the best he could manage was a hazy image of light and dark.

"Out, I said."

He felt the toe of a boot in his ribs. Better there than his balls, he reasoned with himself. One of them had been fond of kicking the balls, and a man who is handcuffed and thrown on the floor can do little to protect those important parts.

"Up, damn you."

He tried. This time he did try to get up. He got as far as his knees, but that was the best he could manage. And that pissed him off. The thought that the son of a bitch jailer might think Custis Long was kneeling to him was too much.

That galvanized him into motion and brought him the rest of the way onto his feet.

He was swaying and unsteady but at least he was upright. The bastards were not going to see him on his knees, damn them.

"All right. This way. Chief wants to see you, God knows why." The jailer smirked and said, "We'll give you a quick trial, mister, and you'll hang before the end of the week."

Longarm's tongue felt thick—surely they hadn't beaten on that too, he thought—and his jaw ached abominably, but on the third try he got some words out. "Fuck you."

He felt a nightstick thud into his lower back. The impact nearly knocked him down again, but he managed to stay upright. He did not want to give these people any satisfaction.

But, oh, unconsciousness had been pleasant. It would be good to go back there again, he was thinking. Just to sort of . . . fade away and feel nothing.

"Go along now. The chief is waiting."

It took some effort, but he put one foot in front of the other. And then again. And again. Right. Walking. That was how you do it, he remembered.

Longarm could not see where he was walking. He could see light and shadow, not much more.

"In there. No, asshole, to your right. Your right, damn you."

Right. Which way was . . . oh, yeah. The right. He

remembered now. He turned to his right, saw brighter light, which suggested an open door, and headed toward it.

He stopped when he bumped up against something that turned out to be the police chief's desk.

He heard the sounds of someone speaking, but at the moment he was concentrating on getting his eyes open a little so that he could see what—and who—was there.

Ah. A man. Civilian suit and tie. Iron-gray hair and mustache. Must be the chief, Longarm assumed.

". . . wanton murder of two of our finest," the chief was saying. "The charges will be first degree . . . What is it, Charles? Don't you know better than to interrupt when I am interrogating a prisoner?"

Interrogating, the man had said, although Longarm did not recall having been asked anything.

Another man, this one wearing a blue uniform, came around behind the desk and whispered into the chief's ear.

"Jesus!" the boss blurted. "I didn't know that. This could be trouble. Big trouble. Get out. Give me a minute to think about this, please."

The policeman hurried away, and Longarm was left standing alone in front of the chief's big desk.

Surely, he thought, this could not get any worse.

Chapter 32

Longarm braced himself for what he feared was about to come. Instead the police chief barked, "Wilson, get the man out of those handcuffs. Barney, bring him a chair. That's right. Set him down easy. Somebody get him some water. Or coffee. Would you like a cup of coffee, Marshal?"

That explained it, Longarm thought. They had taken away his wallet. It seemed someone had bothered to look inside. Probably the son of a bitch opened the wallet thinking to steal whatever money was in it. Instead he'd found the badge.

Good!

"Here, Marshal. Here's a cup of water for you. Steady. Don't spill . . . Help the man, Barney. Help him get a drink there. A drink. Yes. Uh, would you like a little whiskey to, um, brace you up?"

Longarm nodded. He did not feel up to speaking yet, but a nod would do. So would a jolt of whiskey.

The chief fumbled inside his desk drawer and brought out a pint bottle. He pulled the cork and poured a generous measure into the tin cup of water that one of the coppers was holding for him.

The cop held it to Longarm's mouth and tipped some of the watered down whiskey past his lips.

It burned like fire when it hit some previously unsuspected cuts inside his mouth—obviously caused by his own damn teeth when one of the policemen hit him in the mouth—but the warmth spread in his belly once it got down that far.

He nodded his thanks and took a deep breath. The whiskey helped.

"We, um . . . I apologize for my men, Marshal. They may have gotten a little carried away when they thought . . . uh, you know what they thought."

Longarm nodded again.

"After all, two upstanding citizens of this community . . . leading citizens . . . I might even say." The chief stammered.

"An' you," Longarm managed to get out, "were in that asshole McGuire's pocket."

"No, I . . . Certainly not. Absolutely not," the police chief swore.

The man was a liar, of course. Longarm understood that. He also understood that the chief was not likely to admit that to someone else, especially not to a sworn officer of the law. Well, not unless that other someone was also on the take.

"They were just being zealous. No one in this department would do . . . um, would do anything outside the, uh, outside the law." The police chief was sweating. He acted like his collar was two sizes too small and choking him. He kept running a finger inside it and swallowing.

"You're a fucking liar."

Longarm was not exactly sure if he had said those words out loud or if he'd merely thought them.

Things seemed to go dark. His eyes dimmed, and all the sounds around him faded away until there was nothing left.

He felt himself begin to topple over to the side.

He did not feel himself hit the floor.

Chapter 33

"Where am I?" His voice came out as a hoarse croak, but at least he was able to speak. Well, able to whisper anyway.

He felt something stir beside him, and then a woman's voice said, "You passed out. They brought you here."

"Where . . . ," he paused to swallow, which was something not easily done, ". . . is here?"

"Belina's Café," the voice returned. "We're in the back room. That's where I sleep."

"An' who . . . ," he had to swallow again," . . . are you?"

"I'm Belina Jenkins. This is my place."

"Ah. Thanks. How'd I get here?"

"They carried you here."

"Who did?"

"The police. They said you fell down. That's what they always say."

Longarm grunted. He tried to get up, but that was not going to happen. He tried to roll over onto his side. That did not work either. "How'd they know?"

"To bring you here? They knew this was where Tim McGuire's people ran into you. The police always stand watch when McGuire's men are up to something rotten."

"Nice arrangement," Longarm said.

"Convenient," Belina Jenkins agreed. "Can I get you something? You look like you are in pain. I don't have any laudanum, but I do have some powders for," she giggled, "for ladies' disorders."

That brought a smile to his lips. The distortion of his mouth caused some of the little cuts to pull and crack, and it hurt like hell. Even so, it was nice to be able to smile again. "Reckon I'll pass on your powders for ladies then," he said.

"Come morning I can run get you some laudanum," she offered.

"We'll see 'bout that in the morning."

"Close your eyes now. Go back to sleep. It is the best thing for you." She hesitated, then added, "I hope you don't mind if I lie here beside you. This is the only bed I have, and . . ."

"You don't have t' explain nothing. I'm the guest here, not you. I just thank you for helpin' like you are."

"Fine. Hush now. Sleep."

Longarm was not sure, but he thought he felt the light brush of a hand over his sweaty forehead.

He closed his eyes and was almost instantly asleep.

Chapter 34

He woke to the sound of pots rattling, the stove door clanging, and the chatter of customers out in the café. Now that it was daylight, he was able to see a little through the slits that were his eyes at the moment. He seemed to be in a storage room. There were crates and boxes and sacks arranged along the walls and two doors, one that would lead into the café, he supposed, and the other into an alley.

Belina's seemed to be popular now that Big Tim McGuire's people were not coming around to chase people away. Longarm smiled. He had accomplished that much anyway. Hadn't learned a damn thing about Frank Nellis or what happened to Sybil, but at least he had done Belina some good.

He tried once again to sit up. The pain in his belly and side was too much. He probably could have taken the pain if he had to. Fortunately he did not have to. He lay back down and closed his eyes again.

"Can you sit up?"

"Wha . . . Oh, it's you."

"Who did you expect?"

"I dunno. Sorry."

"Don't be. Can you sit up a little? You need something to eat."

At the mention of food, his belly rumbled and growled. It was almost completely dark in the back room. A candle was burning out in the café, but there was no light in the back. Possibly the woman did not trust the threat of an open flame due to the jumble of goods she stored there.

"I don't know," he admitted.

"Try, please. I'll bring some broth that I made for you."

When she returned, she was carrying a saucepan and a spoon. Longarm shook his head and said, "Not possible quite," he winced, "quite yet."

Belina seemed to ponder that for a moment. Then she smiled. "I know what we can do."

She set the saucepan down but took the spoon with her. The next time she came back she was carrying a metal tube with a rubber bulb on one end. "It's a baster," she said. "I use it to suck up the juice from a roast or whatever and squirt it over the meat." She smiled. "I don't see why it can't be used to squirt broth into your mouth."

Belina propped Longarm's head on the pillow, parted the hairs of his mustache, and pressed the small, open end of her baster between his lips.

The first shot was too much for him to swallow. He coughed out half the broth. But the liquid, rich with fats and spices, was almost sinfully good.

"Not so . . . not so much. But it's wonderful."

She tried again, less at a squeeze this time, and Longarm sucked at the baster like he would at a tit. "Damn, that's good."

After she had gotten a cup of broth or more into him, she removed the pillow and said, "That should be enough for now. I don't want to make you sick. You've been empty for a long time."

"Long time?" he asked. "Didn't I have lunch here just today? Or maybe yesterday?"

Belina laughed. "You've been lying here out cold for four days, mister."

"I'll be damned." He closed his eyes and slept again.

Longarm woke to feel the warmth of Belina's plump body beside his, pressing against his side, her hand flung across his chest. He squirmed, trying to find a more comfortable position. The movement—or something—caused her hand to shift. Lower. So that it was lying on top of his cock.

The accidental contact was enough to make his dick swell and grow. In moments he had a rock-hard boner that he tried to will away, not wanting to exceed his welcome in the woman's bed.

It did not work, and in her sleep Belina moved ever so slightly. It had the effect of rubbing his cock.

Longarm's breathing became rapid and shallow, and he felt fairly sure that if he did not wake her or somehow move her hand away, he was going to squirt hot cum all over her hand, his own belly, and the sheet that loosely covered the two of them.

Then he realized that Belina's breathing was rapid too.

She moved. Slid down toward the foot of the bed until her head was at his waist level.

In the darkness he could feel her breath hot on his cock.

She took it in her hand. Peeled his foreskin back.

And took him into the heat of her mouth.

Longarm stroked her head, her back, discovered that she was naked. He began to thrust upward with his hips. That hurt like hell, but he could not control the impulse to drive ever deeper into her mouth.

It was over in moments. Longarm came in a rush. Belina swallowed hard, sucked on him a little longer, then with a sigh lay back down close against his side.

He closed his eyes and again slept.

Chapter 35

He was feeling better. Well enough to leave, actually, after six days flat on his back. But there was something he had to do first.

"Wait a minute, Belina. Before you open up this morning, come here, please."

"What is it, Custis?" She obediently came over to the bedside, her dress in her hand, her underwear stark white against pale, puffy flesh.

He took her hand and pulled her down onto the bed beside him. Each morning and again every evening for the past two days she had favored him with blowjobs. Now he wanted to give something back.

Longarm lifted her chemise and suckled her tits, tantalizing her nipples with his tongue while he kneaded her other tit with a hand.

He squeezed her tit and ran his hand down across her more than ample belly. Belina's body did not excite him, really, but she was a good and generous woman, and he was sure she wanted more of him than she had been taking. Was sure she wanted more than the feel of his dick in her mouth and the taste of his cum.

He ran a finger through the wire-tough curly hairs at her

crotch and found the opening to her pussy. A minute or so of stroking and Belina was wet and already beginning to writhe and moan under his touch.

He pulled her drawers off and levered her legs apart, then shifted his body over hers, lying on top of her. And then in her.

Belina gasped when she felt Longarm's length enter her body. She lifted her hips to him, and he began to slowly pump in and out.

After no more than a minute, Belina cried out and clamped her thighs hard around his hips as she shuddered and gasped in the throes of her climax.

Longarm kept going. Slowly. Then faster, faster still, until he was pummeling her body with his. Faster until he felt the sap rise within his balls and explode outward into Belina's pussy.

She cried out again from her second climax, and he joined her in the sweet release.

Belina held him tight and began to cry.

Longarm pulled back, saw the tears streaking her cheeks. "What's wrong? Did I go an' do something wrong?"

She shook her head violently from side to side. Still crying, she said, "No, Custis, you did nothing wrong. I just . . . I just . . . It was so wonderful. It was everything I hoped it would be. I know . . . I know I'm fat and men don't find me pretty, but you . . . I'm so glad my first time was with you."

"First time?" he asked.

She nodded. "No one has ever cared for me like that before. Oh, I've diddled myself, like with cucumbers and things, and when I was little a boy taught me how to suck a cock. But I've never . . . you know." She smiled through the tears. "Until now." Belina kissed him. "Thank you. Now, please excuse me. I really have to get the café open, dear."

She got up, dressed quickly, and hurried up front to start cooking for the day.

Longarm took his time about getting dressed. It occurred

to him, not for the first time, that he had no idea what had become of his rented mare and the burro with all his things loaded onto it.

He could ask a cop, he thought with a half smile. They seemed to know everything that happened around here, so maybe they would know that too.

Longarm yawned and stretched and went out front so Belina could cook him some breakfast before he left to resume his search for Sybil Nellis.

Before he left the small, dim room where he had been Belina's patient for all these days, he slipped a twenty-dollar double eagle into the pocket of an apron she had hanging there. He knew good and well she would not take pay for what she had done for him, but he had been eating her food—and sharing her bed—for all this time. He thought it only right that she not be out for the cost of all that food.

Chapter 36

"Animals found on the street like that would be impounded and taken to Zuniford's Livery out on the edge of town. The owner can come claim them up to ten days if he pays for their board and impoundment fees. After that they become public property and are sold at auction," the desk sergeant said.

"What about in this case?" Longarm asked.

"All right, what about this case?" the sergeant returned.

"In this case, your officers beat the crap outa me and laid me up so's I couldn't tend to that horse and the burro. I'd think it was the department's responsibility to see to my animals," Longarm said. He was becoming more than a little irritated with these local police.

The sergeant only shrugged and went back to reading a newspaper on his desk.

"I want to see the chief," Longarm said, his voice hardening.

The sergeant looked up. "He don't want to see you."

Longarm headed toward the police chief's office, fully intending to barge in unannounced if he had to. Or by main force if it came to that. He was saved from the necessity by the chief himself who was on his way out somewhere.

"Aw, Long. You, um, look much better than the last time I saw you. What seems to be the problem now?"

When Longarm explained the situation to him, the chief looked at the sergeant who had followed and was standing behind Longarm now—Longarm guessed that was so he could employ his nightstick in an attack from behind; he suspected most of these cops were a sorry lot.

"Jerry, write the man a note." To Longarm he said, "Give the note to Clete Zuniford. The town will pay to house your animals while you were, um, unavailable."

Longarm grunted and turned away. He did not feel any need to thank the chief for simply doing what was right . . . after first the man and his people had been doing what was so very wrong to begin with.

He did, however, collect the note from the desk sergeant. He stuck it into his pocket and headed for the land office, the original reason he had come to town.

Once there, he ran into more officious bullshit.

"I'm sorry, sir. Claim filings are not public record. I can't show them to you." The clerk was a small man who looked to be in his twenties but whose hairline was receding to the point of being nearly bald already. He wore sleeve garters and eyeshades over wire-rimmed spectacles. And he looked almighty pleased with himself to be able to turn down a request by a citizen.

Longarm sighed. If it weren't for Belina Jenkins, he would have been awfully tired of this town. He reached into his pocket and produced his wallet.

The land office clerk's expression brightened. No doubt, Longarm thought, the sorry son of a bitch was thinking he was about to receive a bribe for giving out information that should have been public record anyway.

Instead of paper currency, Longarm produced his badge.

"I ain't the public, mister. Now get those recent filings. And do it right damn now."

The clerk peered down at the badge, then up at Longarm's iron-hard expression and ice-cold eyes. "Yes, sir."

Chapter 37

Clete Zuniford was much more pleasant to get along with than the so-called public servants had been. The man was an aging, stove-up former cowpuncher who used a cane to help support a leg that bent in places where legs should not bend, but that did not seem to slow him down much. It certainly had not made him bitter, like so many invalided punchers Longarm had seen through the years.

"Oh, yes. Fine animals, sir, and I think you will find that they have been well taken care of." He smiled. "I can't abide seeing an animal go hungry or thirsty. They've had all the hay and water they want and," he winked, "they may have gotten a little grain now and then too. Even the little guy."

"Do you have my packs too?" Longarm asked.

"Yes, of course. I put them in my office there so when I wasn't around they were under lock and key. I'm sure nothing was taken. If you do find that anything disappeared while they were in my care, just let me know and I will pay for the missing things."

"If anything did go missing," Longarm said, "I'm betting it would be into the pocket of one of your policemen. My opinion of those folks isn't very good."

Zuniford offered no comment to that, which Longarm

suspected was comment enough in itself. Not that Longarm blamed the man. He lived here and had to do business with those tarnished coppers. If they wanted to, they could make trouble for Zuniford.

"They're in the back there. I'll get them for you," Zuniford said. "You can grab your things out of the office."

Longarm checked his pockets for the map he had purchased at the land office—the miserable little son of a bitch there had made him pay for it—then went in to get his saddle and packs.

There were four different sites that conceivably could have been the Nellis find. The time frame fit if nothing else. And the timing was really all he had to go on. Each had been marked on the map for him. At least the man had done that much without charging extra.

When Zuniford led the mare and the burro in from one of the small corrals behind the livery barn, Longarm saw that both animals were sleek with fat. It was obvious that the man had not only fed them well while Longarm was recuperating from his beating, but also brushed them to a gloss—even the fuzzy-eared burro.

"They look good," Longarm told him, meaning it. "Thank you."

"Oh, they were nice company. I enjoyed having them here."

"You're sure the town will pay for their board?" Longarm asked.

Zuniford nodded. "They will. I have that note you gave me. It will serve as a warrant for payment."

The crippled former cowboy loaded the burro for him while Longarm was busy with his saddle. Built a pack that was tighter and tidier than Longarm could have done too.

When the animals were ready to head out, Longarm said, "Let me check to make sure I didn't miss anything in there." He hadn't and he knew it, but there was one more thing he wanted to do inside Zuniford's office cubicle.

He stepped inside, fished another of his double eagles out of his pocket, and laid it on the liveryman's cluttered desk. He deserved that for the care he had given to those animals.

Finally he stepped into the saddle for the first time in too many days and touched the brim of his Stetson to Clete Zuniford.

A slight squeeze of his legs and the mare stepped out, the little burro following at the end of the lead rope.

Chapter 38

He might as well have entered one of those English mazes like he had read about. The tangle of canyons, gulches, and gulleys was a mass of twists and turns, but Longarm kept reminding himself: Follow the water. All of the creeks and streams branched off the same core. So what he needed to do was follow the water and investigate the side branches one by one. It was tedious but necessary if he wanted to find his way to those minerals claims.

That brought him inevitably back to Bedlam. It was familiar territory, even if it was not remembered with any degree of fondness. Still, it was a place where a man could get a meal and a drink.

Longarm stopped in front of the same familiar tent and dismounted, weary from the travel and—more importantly—from the likelihood of failure. He doubted there was a chance in hell of his being able to find and identify the men who had raided the Nellis claim.

Frank Nellis had surely been killed immediately, and by now the daughter would just as surely have been murdered as well. Once the raiders had their fun with the girl, they would almost certainly have killed her to keep her from talking.

Besides all that, his damn vacation was almost over and he had not had a moment of the rest and relaxation he had been looking forward to.

His fishing pole was still back there on the burro. He had not wet his line a single moment since leaving Denver, and that pissed him off. So his mood was less than good when he walked under the tarp at the front of the cook tent.

The hairy man who was serving up the food today smiled when he saw Longarm. "Liked us so good you couldn't stay away, is it?"

"Yeah, somethin' like that," Longarm grunted. "What do you have to eat today?"

The fellow grinned. "Are you sure you want to know?"

"I'm curious. Hungry too. So what is it?"

"Bear meat," the man said.

"Hell, I've eaten bear before this. Bring it on." He grabbed up one of the tin plates in the washtub and held it out for a large helping of the pungent, greasy stew with chunks of meat, turnips, and carrots. Along with some bits of this and that that he could not identify and thought it probably best to not ask about.

"Tasty," he said after the first bite.

He carried his plate to one of the logs provided for seating, settled there beside the creek, and proceeded to polish off that first plate, then go back and pay for another. The bear meat tasted much like pork, he thought.

"I guess you do like it," the server said. "Say, there's a fella that would like to talk with you. I just remembered."

"All right," Longarm said. "After I eat. What does this man want and where can I find him?"

"He'll tell you himself what he wants. He's in that log outfit down there on the right. It's a mercantile. Ask for Sy."

"All right, thanks." But right now the bear stew took precedence over any conversation.

Chapter 39

Sy Monroe was a middle-aged man with an iron-gray mustache and bright blue eyes over leather-tanned apple cheeks. He was the sort another would meet and immediately feel comfortable with.

"Fella over at the cook tent said you're wanting to speak with me," Longarm said by way of introduction.

"If you are the man who took down Henry Lewis, I do," Monroe said.

"Reckon I'd be him," Longarm admitted.

"Come inside, please. We'll sit and have a drink and talk about a few things."

Longarm followed Monroe into his cluttered general store. The man carried almost everything a man could want—sturdy clothing, cured tobacco, canned milk, shovels and picks and gold pans. His log building was small, but even so it was impressive in the scope of products he offered.

"How in the world did you get all this stuff in here?" Longarm asked. "I don't see no wagons outside."

"I used wagons, of course. I follow the strikes and set up wherever I think a claim has staying power. Some peter out in a few days or a few weeks. I'm betting that Bedlam will last. We'll turn into a real town, just you wait and see."

"And your wagons?"

"I have two of them," Monroe said. "They're busy now hauling ore down to Fort Collins."

"Those must've been yours that I passed on the way up here then," Longarm said.

"Likely," Monroe agreed. "They stay busy traveling back and forth. Ore going down and general freight coming back up." He smiled. "It's all honest business that one of these days will make me a rich man. And no risk even if a mine or a town plays out and goes under."

"You're a thinking man," Longarm said.

"So I be, if I do say so," Monroe said. "I also happen to head our citizens committee. Which is the point of what I wanted to talk with you about, mister."

"All right." Longarm pulled a cheroot out of his jacket. Before he could get a match out of his pocket, Monroe had come up with one of his own. The canny storekeeper snapped the Lucifer aflame and held it for Longarm to light his cigar. "Thanks." Longarm took a long pull on the cheroot, drew the smoke into his lungs, and slowly let it out. "You were saying?"

"I was saying that Bedlam has potential, Mr. Long. It has legs, and our citizens committee has faith in this camp. We want to prosper and we want to grow. In order to do that we need to structure ourselves as a real town. And that means law and order. Are you following me?"

"I certainly agree that Bedlam needs some law and order," Longarm said. "I have some personal reasons to say that, as I reckon you already know."

"Of course. Henry Lewis," Monroe said. He cleared his throat and said, "Mr. Long, our committee has voted to offer you forty dollars a month in cash plus a hut to live in free of charge and found. You would take your meals with Barnabas down the block there. Those would be free of charge too, of course."

"You're sayin' you want me to be your town marshal?" Longarm asked.

"Exactly." Monroe smiled. "We don't have a badge for you to wear, but I can order one out of the Sears catalog. In the meantime we could fashion something that would serve the purpose."

Longarm laughed. And pulled out his wallet. "Something like this one here?"

Monroe leaned forward to peer at the badge Longarm displayed. Then he rocked back on his heels. "You are . . . ?"

"Uh-huh," Longarm said. "I'm a deputy U.S. marshal. I happen to be on vacation right now, though you wouldn't know that from the way things are goin' for me lately, but, yes, I am one. I work for Billy Vail down in Denver."

"I guess you think our offer pathetic then."

"Not at all," Longarm told the man. "Fact is, I'm flattered that you would think of me, and I hope you'll find someone to take the job and do it justice for you. And for Bedlam."

Monroe sighed. "I will tell the committee, of course."

"If there is anything I can do for you . . . short of wearin' your badge, that is . . . just ask."

"You already did quite a lot for us when you killed . . . defended yourself from Henry Lewis. Bedlam is a nicer place for it."

"The man was, um, something of a nuisance, I'd guess," Longarm said.

"That and then some," Monroe agreed.

"Say, while I'm right here, d'you have any good jerky I could buy?"

Monroe the town committeeman immediately turned into Monroe the salesman. "I have some of the best," he said, rubbing his hands together. "Deer, elk, or bear. No beef, I'm afraid. No point in hauling it all the way up here when we can make all we need from the mountains around us. And for you . . . my best price."

"Elk jerky then. Five pounds of it. An' a sack o' rice. And coffee. I'm a little low on coffee too. I'll look around while you're getting those together and see if I can think of anything else I need."

Chapter 40

Two days out of Bedlam, and after three false starts into drainages that were not what he wanted, Longarm found the first of the claims noted on the Fort Collins land office clerk's map.

It was a hardscrabble outfit if Longarm ever saw one. It consisted of a Sibley tent set up on a bench beside the waters of a small stream, along with a tarp strung on what was left of some tree trunks after the tops had been harvested for some reason.

The beginnings of a mine showed on the canyon wall above the camp. A trash heap of broken rock spilled down the hillside below the mine opening.

Longarm did not know how many men might have been inside the hole, but he clearly saw the one who set aside the pans he was busy washing and picked up his rifle at the first sight of a stranger approaching.

"That's close enough, mister," the guard called out when Longarm was about thirty yards downstream from the claim. "Halt and state your business."

"Passing through, that's all," Longarm shouted back to the man.

The fellow was lean and shaggy. It looked like it had been

weeks since he'd had a shave, longer since his last haircut. He was hatless and dressed in bib overalls but no shirt and no shoes.

"You're alone?"

"I am," Longarm shouted. "I don't mean you no harm. Mind if I come in an' climb down off'n this animal for a while? It would feel awful good to stretch my legs and have a human person to talk to. I ain't had nobody but these two animals to visit with for days, and they don't say much."

The guard laughed and said, "All right then. Come ahead."

But Longarm noticed that the fellow did not set his rifle aside.

Longarm nudged the mare with his heels and the sturdy horse moved forward. He reined to a halt near the tarpaulin fly and dismounted there. He tied the mare to one of the stakes holding a guy rope for the tarp and left the burro's lead rope tied to the horn on his saddle.

He introduced himself—by name but not by occupation—and got back, "Charles Jones. I'm one of the owners here."

One of the owners, Longarm already knew from the claim filing, along with Jerry Wilson, Thomas Wilson, Randall Oakes, and Cory Bettencort.

"Light and have a cup of calico tea if you like," Jones offered. "We're all out of coffee, but we have a little tinned milk left to make the calico tea." He smiled. "It ain't bad once you get used to it, even without sugar, which we also run out of."

"Oh, I've been down to calico a time or two," Longarm said. It was the truth. And the stuff was not awful. At least it was hot and filled a man's belly. "I thank you for the offer, but I'll pass for now. No offense, I hope."

"None taken," Jones said. "I don't suppose you'd sell that burro, would you? Me and my partners walked in. Had us a burro of our own, but something took and ate it. Catamount, maybe, or a bear."

"How do you figure to get your ore out when you want to sell it?" Longarm asked, genuinely curious.

Jones shrugged. "Pack it out on our own backs, whatever ones of us go down to civilization. That should pay enough that we can buy some animals. And some supplies. Say, you wouldn't have any coffee or beans or anything you'd sell to us, would you? We don't have much in the way of cash, but we'd pay what we could."

"Reckon I could share with you," Longarm said, looking around for horse droppings. Jane Nellis had made it clear that the men who raided their claim had come on horseback. She had mentioned something about their animals. And the fact that they had two packhorses with them.

That information pretty much ruled out Charles Jones and partners as the Nellis raiders.

"I have a little coffee here too if it would help," he said.

"Coffee? Lord, mister, any one of us would kill for a cup of coffee," Jones said.

Longarm chuckled and said, "Let me dig some out o' my pack then an' we'll brew up a pot. How are you fixed for eatables? I got a little rice I could share, I think, an' some cornmeal."

"Mister, you are a godsend," Jones said, setting the rifle aside and coming eagerly forward. He turned, cupped his hands to his mouth, and called, "Hey, boys. Coffee. We got coffee a-brewing down here. You'd best come quick or I'll damn sure drink it all."

He was grinning broadly when he turned back to face Longarm.

Chapter 41

Jones and his partners were a pleasant bunch. Young, all of them, and determined to make their fortune in mining. Longarm saw the quality of their ore—silver—and suspected this mine would not be the basis of anyone's fortune.

But one find was not necessarily the end of the road for their hopes. When this claim petered out—and he suspected that it would—he felt sure these boys had the determination to pick up and move on. Searching. Scrambling. He hoped they would fulfill their dreams. Eventually. Not here, perhaps, but eventually.

He left them with half his coffee and a third of his rice but declined their invitation to stay the night in their camp.

That was only partially because he did not want to eat what little they had to offer.

Mostly it was because he was uncomfortable lying down to sleep among strangers. A man just never knew . . .

Longarm shared a cup of java with the boys, then wished them well and swung into the saddle again.

"I have an hour or so of daylight. Reckon I'd best use it. Say, you haven't run across any other fellas out this way, have you?"

"We haven't done any wandering," Tom Wilson told him.

Wilson was a lean scarecrow of a man, his brother Jerry looking like a twin despite a two-year difference in their ages. Wilson smiled ruefully and said, "If we wanted to walk, we'd walk down to Bedlam for some supplies. You said it's a couple days by horseback? Think what that hike would be for us without no horse nor even a burro."

"What you need," Longarm said, "is mules, but they come awful dear. An' that's to say nothing 'bout feeding them." He looked around. "There sure ain't much for an animal to eat on around here. Nothing but rock."

"Yeah, but rock is where you find the mineral," the other Wilson said. "Are you sure you won't stay the night?"

Nice fellows. But Longarm had the sneaking suspicion that they would like to have his horse and burro.

He touched the brim of his Stetson in farewell.

And touched a spur to the side of the mare. She and her fuzzy-eared friend moved out smartly, and the first of the four mines on his map was quickly left behind.

Chapter 42

The second mine was named the A.M., filed on and registered to a Jonas Morgan.

Once he became better oriented by finding the Jones outfit, Longarm had an easier time of finding the A.M.

It very quickly became apparent that this had nothing to do with Frank Nellis or the raiders who killed him. The M in the mine's name stood for Morgan and the A for his wife Alva.

The outfit was being worked by just the two of them, Jonas doing the digging and Alva providing what was really a fairly nice home for him there under the canvas of their tents, one for sleeping and the other for storage and cooking.

Alva had fixed it all up. She'd even found some decorative leafs somewhere on the hills around them and arranged those like they were flowers.

There were no windows to put curtains on, but Longarm was sure the lady would have hung some if she'd only had windows.

Jonas was a husky man, probably in his late thirties. His wife was short and scrawny. Both had coal-black hair. Longarm hesitated to guess Alva's age—it was something he did badly—but if held to, he would have pegged her at at least ten years younger than Jonas.

They were a friendly and welcoming couple, seemingly with no worry that they might be raided, just the two of them so far from any form of civilization.

Longarm was sure they had a rifle or a shotgun tucked away somewhere. After all, they had fresh meat that they were willing to share. But neither one of them reached for a weapon when he rode up on their camp.

He hoped that trust in their fellow man would not backfire on them sometime in the future.

"Light and set, mister," Alva said. "I'll call my man down to meet you." She smiled and wiped her hands on her apron. "We get to see so few folks out this way. Here, let me get him."

She gathered up her skirts and scampered up the hillside to their mine, which even from down beside a thin, probably seasonal creek Longarm could see was properly shored up and well constructed. He noticed that Alva left their possessions unguarded and seemed to have no concern about that.

When Jonas came down with her to meet their visitor, the man was smiling and had his hand outstretched to shake before he was within ten paces of Longarm.

"You'll stay and eat with us, won't you?" the man said as soon as the introductions were complete. "Alva does wonders with venison pot roast and wild onions." He smacked his lips and added, "Magnificent."

"I'd be honored," Longarm said. "Mind if I unsaddle and let the mare have a little relief."

"Please do. Put her and the little fellow up the canyon with our boys, if you like. There's some wild hay that I gathered. Give them each an armful of that. You will stay the night, won't you?"

It was still no later than mid-afternoon, but Longarm found himself nodding agreement. He dropped his bedroll off his pack and considered what he might offer to them in exchange for their hospitality. He would have to decide that in the morning. This afternoon he probably could get an idea of what they lacked. Although at first look, Jonas and Alva Morgan seemed to have prepared themselves very well for a long and, he hoped, a prosperous stay.

The "boys" tied on a picket rope above a twist in the canyon proved to be three stout, handsome mules. Yes, Jonas had prepared well.

The mules gave him a curious look when he showed up leading the mare and the burro, but they did not offer to fight.

Longarm swept up an armload of wild hay from a large pile and dropped it in front of his animals, then stripped the saddle and the pack from the two of them.

He spent a few minutes currying them and checking their feet before returning to the Morgans' tent.

Alva already had a pot of coffee on the fire and a larger pot of meat simmering.

"Welcome," Jonas said. "Now, sit, please, and tell us what is going on in the world outside. We haven't heard nor seen a thing in the past three months, so any news you can tell us would be greatly appreciated."

Chapter 43

"You might be surprised," Jonas said over the rim of his coffee cup—crockery, not tin—as he squatted on a home-made stool. "There are more people in these hills and more minerals claims than you might think. And not all of the claims are ever filed. It is too far down to the nearest land office for folks to file papers unless they are sure of what they have. Sometimes not then too."

He pursed his lips and looked at his wife. "So many of these finds don't prove worthwhile, you see. A man will dig for two, three months. Maybe the work will pay off. More often than not it's a waste. But if you don't try, well, you don't hit your strike. It's all a big gamble."

"What about you?" Longarm asked. "Is this find going to pay out for you?"

Again Jonas looked at his wife, but this time he did not immediately answer.

Longarm smiled, suspecting what it was that made the man hesitate. "I haven't seen cause to mention it before now," Longarm said, "but I'm a deputy U.S. marshal. I ain't after gold or silver or anything else that comes out o' the ground."

"Do you have credentials to prove that?" Jonas asked.

"Sure." Longarm dug into his pocket and produced his

wallet and badge. He handed them across the fire to Jonas and accepted a refill of coffee from Alva. He stirred some canned milk and a little wild honey into the coffee.

Jonas looked at Alva and got a nod from her before he handed the wallet back. Then he smiled. "This one will pay out," he said. "In another year or so we'll need to put a road in so we can haul ore down to a crusher and smelter. But that won't be for a while, of course."

"You seem to know your business," Longarm observed.

"I should. I studied geology and mineral sciences at Pennsylvania State College," Jonas said proudly.

"That's where you're from? Pennsylvania?" Longarm asked. He still had a nagging disregard for Pennsylvania due to his West Virginia roots.

"Both of us are," Jonas said. "We're from a small burg, more of a hamlet really, called Needmore." He grinned. "Nobody's ever heard of it except us and the folks who still live there."

"Oh, that ain't so. I heard of it. Used to know a fella that came from there."

Jonas raised an eyebrow, so Longarm added, "His name was . . . let me think, it's been a while . . . his name was Beavers. Loyce Beavers."

"I don't know anybody named Loyce, but I went to grammar school with a boy named Charlie Beavers. Likely they'd be kin. So tell us what you're doing up here, Deputy."

"Lookin' for some men that raided a mining camp. They kidnapped a girl an' likely killed the owner."

"Oh? I don't like the sound of that," Jonas said.

"What are their names?" Alva put in.

"Nellis," Longarm said. "The man's name is Frank Nellis."

"Does he have a wife named Jane?" Alva asked.

"Matter o' fact, yes. She got away. Right now she's down in Silver Plume recovering from a gunshot wound," Longarm said.

"Oh, the poor dear. Jonas, you remember them, don't you? Frank and Jane? I'm pretty sure their name is Nellis."

"You've met them?" Longarm began to feel a flutter of excitement in his gut, the excitement of the chase.

"Yes, we have," Jonas said. "They passed through here a couple months back."

"A lovely couple," Alva said. "And that girl." She did not sound so enthusiastic when she mentioned Sybil.

"Nice folks, Frank and Jane," Jonas affirmed. But he did not mention the daughter at all.

"Do you have any idea where they were bound?" Longarm asked.

Jonas shook his head. "I'm sorry, no. They were on their way in when we met them. I can tell you where we advised them to go."

"But we don't know if they went there," Alva said.

"It's worth a try," Longarm told them. He leaned back and accepted the steaming bowl of stew that Alva handed him. The scent rising from it made his mouth water. And the taste of it bettered the scent. "Ma'am, this has to be the best stew this side o' Denver." He grinned. "Maybe the best this side o' Needmore, Pennsylvania."

He meant every word of it.

Chapter 44

After supper, Longarm walked with Jonas into the side canyon so they could water the livestock and see that there was plenty of hay available to them. Then the two men sat beside the creek and smoked a pair of Longarm's cheroots.

They sat there smoking and idly talking about Pennsylvania and West Virginia—neither had been back in years, Longarm not in considerably longer a time than Jonas—while the evening came down over the mountains.

A herd of seven mule deer drifted down to drink from the thin run of water.

"There isn't an evening," Jonas said in a subdued voice, "that I couldn't knock down a deer or an elk or sometimes one of those curly horned mountain sheep. It's fine up here. The only thing we lack is roads and people." He smiled. "Which is one of the best things about it."

He finished his cigar and tossed the butt into the water, then stood, brushing off his britches. "Ready?"

Longarm got up too and the two men walked back to the camp.

Longarm spread his bedroll on the ground inside Alva's cooking tent and told his hosts good night, then lay down and was instantly asleep.

Come morning he asked Jonas, "Which way did the Nellis family head from here?"

Jonas pointed. "I don't know exactly where they went, but that's the direction we advised them to go. We prospected up there a little bit last fall. Found a little molybdenum and what might have been a trace of copper. This find seems the better of the two, so we told Nellis about the moly. I . . . The truth is, I don't think Frank Nellis knew enough about minerals to recognize molybdenum, but he might have figured out the copper."

"Don't even think about leaving us before you have some breakfast," Alva warned.

Longarm grinned. "Wouldn't think of it, ma'am."

Breakfast was more of the excellent venison stew. Longarm had two bowls of it and would have eaten more if he'd thought he could hold it without incurring a bellyache from overstuffing himself.

"If I was a rich man," he said, "I'd hire you t' do my cooking."

"What about me?" Jonas asked.

The grin returned. "You could wash the lady's dishes."

"I see where I stand," Jonas said, smiling.

Longarm stood and dropped his bowl into the washbasin. "Folks, you're both wonderful. Thank you for all you done."

"Head off like I told you," Jonas said. "I'm thinking you might find Frank Nellis's diggings up that way."

"I'm fixing to find out," Longarm said. He rolled and tied his bedroll, then carried it to the mare and the burro, Jonas coming with him to toss some feed to his mules.

Once Longarm was saddled and his pack reloaded onto the burro, the two shook hands and Longarm got onto the trail.

He was several miles away before he remembered that he had not offered Jonas Morgan anything in exchange for the food and hospitality.

He kicked himself much of that morning for the oversight.

Chapter 45

The sky clouded up with rain-laden gray that afternoon, and a wind kicked up out of the northwest. A sudden chill made Longarm dismount and fetch his heavy coat from its perch atop the burro. The temperature must have dropped a good thirty degrees, he suspected.

Standing in his stirrups and craning his neck, he sent worried glances into the face of the wind.

There was a storm brewing, and it would be on him soon.

Colorado mountain storms could be violent if often brief, and Longarm saw no point in riding through this one.

He thought wistfully of Alva Morgan's cook tent, where he had spent the past night, but it was many miles and many hours behind him now.

Instead he thought it sensible to look for a place where he could hole up until the storm blew itself out.

Fat raindrops and a scattering of hailstones were falling by the time be spotted a deep overhang on the rock face above him. He reined the mare into a stand of young aspen and tied her there, then untied the burro from his saddle horn and tied it separately.

"Now, you children mind your manners till I get back,"

he admonished them, before he scrambled up the loose rock slope to the shelter offered by that overhang.

The niche was deeper than it had first appeared. About four feet high at the mouth, it leveled off about two feet tall and extended so far back into the rock that he could not see the back wall.

Longarm chose a spot close to the lip and settled into a comfortable, cross-legged position. From there he could stay out of the storm while at the same time keeping an eye on his animals.

Having not bothered to stop for lunch, he munched on a handful of jerky while he watched the quick flurry of hail and listened to the strong drumming of large raindrops.

Both mare and burro turned their butts to the wind and tucked their tails in tight. Had his niche in the rock been more accessible, Longarm would gladly have shared his shelter with the animals, but that was not possible here.

When he was finished eating, he gathered up a handful of hailstones that had bounced inside his shelter. He popped them into his mouth one by one and let them melt to wash his lunch down. A man could hardly find purer water than that.

Finally he lighted a cheroot and sat back to enjoy the show of nature's fury.

The cigar, it turned out, may well have been a mistake. Perhaps the smoke, but then possibly the cheroot had nothing to do with it.

Whatever the cause, Longarm heard a low, rolling rumble somewhat like the purring of a cat.

A very *big* cat.

Then the mountain lion hit him from behind and bowled him over, the two of them in a tangle tumbling end over end down the rocky slope.

Chapter 46

"Oh, God, I'm blind," he moaned.

"Don't be silly," a voice responded. "Your eyes are caked shut with mucus that accumulated while you were asleep."

"Who the hell?" He tried to sit up but was held back by a hand on his chest.

"Lie still," the voice—a woman's voice—said. "I'll get some warm water to bathe those eyes."

He heard a rustle of cloth, then footsteps. Moments later she returned and he felt the brush of a wet cloth over his face. She scrubbed at his eyes—rather hard, he thought— and his left eye popped open. He strained a little and was able to open the right eye too.

He was in a cabin, lying on a soft mattress, looking up at the heavy beams of the ceiling and at a thin woman with graying hair pulled back in a severe bun. She was wearing a man's red-and-black checked woolen shirt, denim trousers held up by canvas suspenders that he recognized as army issue, and knee-high lace-up boots.

"Who are you?" he asked.

"My name is Katherine Jennings. That is Katherine with a K, please, but you may call me Kat."

Longarm raised an eyebrow, and she smiled. "No, I am not the cat that chased you out of her den yesterday."

"Yesterday?" he asked, his voice coming out as a weak croak.

Kat nodded. "She wasn't trying to kill you. She didn't really think of you as food. She just wanted you away from her babies. She has two of them, the cutest little kittens you ever saw." She smiled again. Katherine Jennings had a lovely smile, in fact, wide and happy and reaching all the way into her eyes.

Then she laughed. "You are so lucky. She didn't like being out in that rain and hail. That's why she left you so quickly and ran back to her babies."

"You . . . How would you know all this?" he asked.

"I am up here researching a paper for the national wildlife service. I've been living here since last winter. I spend most of my time in a blind that the wildlife here has come to accept as normal and nonthreatening. I was here when the kittens were born. I've watched them trying to learn how to hunt. Watched their mama bring live prey home for them to learn on. It is really wonderful the way nature takes care of her own."

"If you say so," Longarm mumbled. Hell, he hadn't known there *was* any sort of national wildlife service. "You say the lion didn't really want t' hurt me?"

"That is not exactly what I said, mister. I said she wanted to chase you away, but it would have been quite all right if she had killed you. From her point of view, that is, not mine. As it is, you were very lucky. That heavy vest you were wearing kept her from ripping your lungs out. A panther's hind foot claws are very powerful, you know. Because of the vest, however, she only scratched you in three places. Of course it remains to be seen whether those wounds will fester and turn green. A cat's claws are quite filthy, you know."

"That's more'n I want t' know," he said. "You say I was clawed?"

"Yes. But I brought you back here, you and your animals. I washed your wounds and put salve on them. It is too soon to know if they will turn bad."

"If they do?" he asked.

"Then you shall die, of course."

"I wouldn't much like that," Longarm said.

Kat smiled. "Then by all means, let's make sure it does not happen."

"When will I know?" he asked.

"Give it three days. I should be able to tell by then."

Longarm nodded. "I might not be real good company for the next couple days."

"That is all right. People say I am not good company anytime. I prefer solitude to the incessant yammering of most people."

Longarm took that as a suggestion. He closed his eyes and tried to go back to sleep.

Chapter 47

Longarm learned two things that afternoon. One was that Kat Jennings was a truly awful cook. The meal she prepared for him would have tasted better if she had simply put the ingredients into a bowl, raw, and given them to him that way.

The other thing was that the woman was not shy. Late in the afternoon she pulled her clothes off, poured a basin of cold water, and proceeded to bathe herself with a tattered sponge.

Longarm pretended not to watch. But he did, fascinated.

The woman was a collection of bones with a meager coating of skin stretched tight over it.

He had never seen any human creature in such a condition.

Hell, any sensible farmer would have rejected her if she applied to become a scarecrow.

Her hip bones stuck out like plowshares, and her chest was a ladder of bone and gristle.

Her tits were like pancakes that had nipples perched atop them. Thin cakes, at that.

Her pussy appeared to be normal enough, topped by a bush that was growing on the flat that separated her skinny thighs. Longarm would have wagered he could put his hands completely around those thighs. They were thinner than most women's calves. Hell, they were thinner than some women's ankles.

And her belly. Flat as a board, it did not begin to belly out.

He gave up pretending to be asleep and sat up on the side of the bed where she had somehow pulled, pushed, or dragged him, never mind that he probably weighed twice what she did. Or more.

He reached for his things, which she had laid out on a stool beside the bed, and picked up a cheroot and a lucifer.

"Oh, you're awake," she said with a smile as soap suds dripped from her pussy hair. Then she went back to scrubbing.

He flicked the match aflame with his thumbnail and applied the fire to the tip of the cheroot. Lord, that was one skinny woman. He had seen mop handles with fuller bodies than that.

Longarm pulled the smoke deep into his lungs, then blew out a series of smoke rings.

Kat finished washing, dried herself off on a piece of burlap, and pulled her clothes on.

"Do you feel up to walking a little?" she asked.

Longarm nodded. He felt perfectly well except for some pain in his right shoulder blade and in the small of his back.

"Good. Those animals of yours need to be let out so they can graze. I don't keep any feed up here. It's too costly. And I can't take the time to mow wild hay, so I just don't have any livestock of my own. I tied yours to some trees down by the creek. They should be safe there unless a grizzly comes along. If that were to happen, they wouldn't be safe in a pen, probably not in a shed either. Grizzlies don't have much respect for mankind or our wants and needs."

"Ain't that the truth," Longarm said. He himself was as naked as Kat had just now been. He gathered that she had stripped his clothing so she could nurse him.

There seemed to be no point in becoming modestly shy

at this late date so he simply stood and dressed. He felt twinges in his back but nothing serious.

It was worrisome, though. He had seen the ugliness of gangrene. And since the clawing had been on his back, amputation, the normal cure for gangrene, was not an option.

If the wounds festered, he would die. Plain and simple.

He stamped into his boots and went outside to find his mare and burro and tend to them.

Chapter 48

After a supper that was every bit as awful as her lunch had been, Kat again stripped Longarm, then rolled him onto his stomach. She leaned over him and pulled away the gauze that she had used to cover his scratches.

"Mm."

"What's that supposed t' mean?" he asked.

"What is?"

"You went 'mm' when you looked at my back."

"Did I?"

"Yes, dammit, you did. So what is 'mm' supposed to mean?"

"Nothing to do with your wounds, actually. I was, uh, remarking unconsciously about your muscle tone. Most men are quite flabby, you know. I can't abide flab. You have excellent muscle tone."

He did not know what to say about that, so he kept his mouth shut.

Kat rubbed something smelly onto his wounds and again plastered them with gauze.

"On your back now, please," she said.

Longarm rolled over, his discomfort less than he might have expected.

Kat's attention shifted below his belt. Or where his belt would have been had he been wearing anything.

It occurred to him to wonder why the woman thought it necessary to completely strip him when it was only his back that had suffered the scratches.

"Would you mind?" she asked.

Longarm did not know what the hell she was asking him about, but he was the guest here and knew a little about proper manners for a guest in someone's home. "No, I don't mind," he said.

Kat smiled hugely. Then stood upright and began stripping.

He at first assumed she was just going to bathe herself again.

Then, still smiling, she crawled onto the bed next to him.

And took his cock into her hand.

Chapter 49

That muff of dark, curly hair hid a pussy that was hot, wet, and deep. Talented too.

Kat rolled on top of him, straddling his waist with those chicken-leg thighs. He was fairly certain her legs could serve a man as pipe stems. If he happened to smoke a pipe, that is.

She pulled his dick into position, then lowered herself onto it.

Longarm groaned and arched his back to meet her, to drive all the deeper into her. "Jeez, woman, that's good."

"Better for me than for you, I wager," she said. "I haven't been with a man for five months." She laughed. "And a carrot just isn't the same."

"You would really . . . ?"

"Of course," she said and gestured toward his cock. "Wouldn't you play with this if it had been that long? Of course you would. What makes you think a woman's needs are any less than yours?"

"I never thought of it that way," he said.

"Shut up and pay attention. You have a huge dick, so be still and let me enjoy myself here."

"Be still?" he said.

"I didn't mean that literally. I mean just shut up and pay attention to business here."

"Well in that case," he said. And began to stroke up and down. Slowly at first, just enjoying the heat of her scrawny body. Then faster. Straining to go ever deeper, ever harder.

Kat responded almost immediately, her breathing coming quicker and her pussy becoming even wetter. Her thighs began to tremble and shake. At first Longarm thought she was overtired and about to collapse. Instead it seemed she was beginning to have an orgasm. A powerful one.

When she came the first time, she cried out and dug her hands painfully into his arms. The second time, which happened only seconds later, she shrieked. And the third time her eyes rolled back in her head and she passed out cold.

The woman was so slight that Longarm scarcely felt her weight on top of him.

Not that he minded. He needed a warm blanket on the high country nights, and a living, breathing, self-heated blanket worked just fine.

Longarm reached his own climax, his cum spurting deep inside Katherine Jennings.

His cock still lodged inside her, he closed his eyes and went comfortably to sleep.

Chapter 50

"I could get used to this," Longarm said as he settled down to a plate of Kat's flannel cakes—that tasted pretty much like actual flannel instead of pancakes—but with a cup of morning coffee. And that made up for all manner of other things; there simply is not much that can compare with a steaming cup of coffee at dawn.

The woman was waiting on him hand and foot. Pampering him outrageously. Apparently she liked having a dick to play with.

"Of course you could," Kat said. "All men are essentially lazy. It's women who do all the work. All you men do is go out once in a while and drag home some meat. Surely you have noticed."

"Can't say that I have," he said. "But then I haven't been looking." He grinned. "Been too busy out there collectin' meat. Say, this coffee is good."

Kat laughed. "Coffee is the only thing I know how to make that is worth spit. I don't care about food, which is probably why I am such a terrible cook . . . No, don't try to be polite. I know the truth. I am a lousy cook. It's coffee that sustains me, not food. But I do love my coffee. Are you done eating?"

He nodded. He hadn't filled his belly, but he would just as soon have chewed off a chunk of his sheepskin vest as have had any more of those flannel cakes.

"Bring your cup and come with me."

"Where?"

"Out there," she said, grabbing him by the arm and pulling him away from the table. "I want to show you something."

"Show me? Woman, it's still dark out there."

"Oh, don't be such an old woman. I know the path, daylight or dark. Now, come along. We have to get up there before it is too late."

Longarm sighed. But he got up and went along with her, each of them carrying a cup of the good coffee.

"Out there" proved to be more "up there." Kat led him up a steep, winding path, probably a sheep trail, to the top of a high knob of rock that hung poised above her cabin.

"Now what?" he asked.

"Sit. Wait."

He sat. And waited. Sipping his coffee slowly and enjoying the aroma of it in the crisp, cold morning air.

Then he saw. The most glorious sunrise he had ever seen, streaks of red and gold across a cloudless eastern horizon. Or perhaps it was simply that this sunrise he could watch, coffee in hand, with no responsibilities weighing on him.

If he had nothing but these few minutes, his vacation was complete.

Kat nudged his elbow and whispered. "Look down there."

She pointed below them to the creek and beyond it. In the golden glow of the early morning he saw a huge cat and two roly-poly kittens emerge from a patch of scrub oak. The mother lion sprawled placidly beside the creek while her babies stalked each other through the grass, pouncing and biting and rolling over and over.

"Is that the cat that . . . ?" he began.

Kat nodded. "She's the one who drove you out of her home. Beautiful, isn't she?"

She was. He had to admit it. The beast was magnificent. And her cubs were like kittens anywhere. Except bigger.

"If I had a rifle . . . ," he said.

"If you did, I would club you with it before I would let you hurt her." Kat sniffed her disapproval. "Men!" she declared.

Longarm chuckled softly, and Kat said, "You were teasing me, weren't you?"

"Hell, of course I was. Why don't we go back down? I dunno about you, but I've finished my coffee an' I'm commencing t' get cold. Let's go on down. You can take a look at my back, and we can fuck. Morning fucks can be the best, y'know."

"Really?"

"Guaranteed."

"Prove it," she challenged, laughing softly.

Longarm stood and took Kat's hand, leading her back down to the warmth of the cabin. And to the bed there.

Chapter 51

They lay in bed, the two of them twined together on a mattress meant for only one. Longarm did not know about Kat, but he was damn near exhausted. The woman was vigorous in the sack, he had to give her that. She climaxed four times to his one and would have happily gone for more if Longarm had only asked.

"So tell me what brings you to this distant part of the landscape, Custis Long?" she asked, her lips tickling his chest hair when she spoke.

"Well, first off, I'm a deputy U.S. marshal. And I'm up here hoping to find out what happened to a girl that was kidnapped somewhere hereabouts."

"Really?" She began licking his left nipple.

He told her. About Frank and Jane Nellis and about their missing daughter, Sybil.

While he was talking, Kat was licking her way across his chest, down his belly, and onto his cock.

Longarm's pecker began to rise to the occasion. He was fairly sure he could make it one more time before he collapsed in utter exhaustion.

Kat lifted her head, spittle glistening on her lower lip. She said, "Did you say Sybil?"

"I did," he grunted.

She shook her head. "That isn't a very common name."

"No, it isn't." He wished she would get back to what she had been doing, running her tongue around and around the head of his prick.

"There is a girl two drainages over. Her name is Sybil. She and her man and his two friends. They are newcomers up here. Only been there a month or so."

Longarm sat upright, dislodging Kat. She nearly fell off the bed. Did fall off him.

His erection faded and he jumped up off the bed completely. He began pulling on his clothes.

"Where are you going?" Kat asked. She sounded disappointed.

"That could be them, Kat. The bunch I'm after. That could be them over there. I have to go at least find out." He stamped into his boots and pulled his gunbelt around his middle. "You got to tell me how to get there."

"Is that more important than . . . Oh, of course it is," she said. She got up, naked as a pile of bones, and headed for the stove. "At least I can send you off with something warm in your belly." She smiled. "If you can stand my cooking one more time, that is."

"I'll just grab some o' those leftover flannel cakes and go," he said. He did not mention that he only wanted to make her feel that she had helped. Those pancakes would find some hungry birds somewhere along the trail.

Longarm dressed quickly, went out and saddled the mare and loaded the burro, then led them up close to the cabin. Kat came out, still bare-ass naked, and gave him a sloppy wet kiss good-bye.

"You're welcome here anytime, Custis Long."

He pinched her nipple, then turned to the mare. "Two drainages, you said?"

"That's right. Due west from here. Sybil's place is on a bench above a dry creek bed. Look for the smoke from her fire to guide you in." Kat laughed. "I ate lunch there just four days ago. The child is an even worse cook than I am."

Longarm kissed the woman again, then swung into the saddle.

There could not possibly be more than one girl named Sybil running around the mountains up here, he thought. This had to be the outfit he was looking for.

Chapter 52

It took him that day and half of the next, but he found what he was sure had to be Frank Nellis's diggings. It was, like Kat had said, on a bench lying above a stream and consisted of a tent and a hole being dug into the side of the mountain.

"Hello," Longarm called from a good distance out. "Is anybody there? Hello?"

A girl with long, unkempt hair came out of the tent. She looked like she had been napping in there. She wore a shapeless shift that looked more like a slip than a dress. If this indeed was Sybil Nellis, she was sixteen years old, but she looked more like fourteen.

"Hello," Longarm said, approaching her. "I haven't had a soul t' talk to for days. I wonder, could I buy a meal from you? I can pay."

"Cash money?" a man's voice called from inside the hole in the ground.

"Cash money," Longarm affirmed, stepping down from the mare without waiting for an invitation. "I can pay you a dollar."

The man stepped out of his adit and said, "Let's see your money then."

Longarm smiled. He found a silver dollar in his pockets,

walked over to the diggings, and handed the coin to the man, who then leaned to the side and called out, "Give him something to eat, Sybil."

"Sybil, huh? Unusual name."

The fellow ignored that, so Longarm added, "Is she your daughter?"

That brought the man's head snapping around toward Longarm again. "She's my woman, and don't you be messing with her."

"Whoa. No offense intended," Longarm said. "I was just makin' conversation."

"We don't need no conversation. You paid for a meal, not to talk."

"Of course," Longarm said. "My name, by the way, is Long, Custis Long." He held a hand out in an offer to shake. The man ignored it.

Longarm smiled anyway. He led his animals down to the creek and allowed them to drink, then tied them to some nearby brush and went back up to the tent where Sybil—he was convinced she had to be Sybil Nellis, but he had no proof of it—was frying some pan bread over a folding sheepherder stove.

He hunkered down close to where she was working and took out a cheroot. He nipped the twist off, struck a match, and lighted the cigar. Exhaling a puff of smoke, he said, "Sybil, huh? Nice name. What is you folks' last name?"

She looked at him. She had a small, pouty, little girl mouth and bushy eyebrows. "Are you always this nosy?"

Longarm smiled. "Matter o' fact, I am. I'm just curious about most everything. That's what brings me out into these hills. Curiosity, that's what. So what is y'all's last name, anyhow?"

"Not that it is any of your business, but my name is Nellis. My man in there is Harry Carver."

And there it was. Nellis. Out of her own mouth, it was confirmed.

Longarm glanced around to make sure none of the three men had come out of their diggings. He lowered his voice and said, "Your mother sent me, Sybil. I'm here to rescue you from those fellas."

She stood upright, forgetting her pan bread. "You . . . Is that the truth? My mother sent you to get me away from Harry?"

Longarm nodded. "It's true, girl. Now, gather up anything you want to bring with you. I'm taking you to your mama, and I'm promising you that those men that kidnapped you won't bother you no more."

Sybil Nellis took a step forward. Then she drew in a deep breath. And just as loudly as she could she screamed, "Harry! Come quick. This man is the law."

Chapter 53

Harry and two others, all of them blond—and big—came boiling out of the mouth of the diggings.

They were carrying sledgehammers and looked like they intended to use them.

Longarm threw himself backward. He lost his footing and went tumbling end over asshole down the slope toward the creek and his animals.

He hit the creek with a splash and came onto hands and knees shivering—the damned water was ice cold—then crawled out before the men could come down with those hammers. A sledgehammer applied to the skull, or to any part of the body for that matter, could ruin a man's whole day.

If appearances were anything to go by, those three up there on the bench were brothers. They all looked very much alike. And they all looked thoroughly pissed off.

Longarm came up with his .45 in hand.

"Stop right there," he barked.

The rear two stopped. The first man who had come out, the one Longarm took to be Harry, was too angry to have any sense left in his head. Assuming he had had some in there to begin with.

That one kept coming, sledgehammer upraised ready to

strike. Ready to crush Longarm's skull if he allowed Harry to get that close.

"Stop, I'm tellin' you."

It was breath wasted. Harry charged down the slope with blood in his eye.

And soon enough with blood all over his face. Longarm shot him. The heavy slug took him just to the side of the bridge of his nose. Harry's face crumpled inward on itself, and his body no longer had anyone up there controlling it.

He fell in a tangle of arms and legs, the sledgehammer flying off to the side, and his lifeless body slid down into the water.   •

The other two spun on their heels and ran back inside their hole in the ground.

Sybil stood staring down at the man who had taken her.

Before the girl had time enough to gather her wits, Longarm ran up the slope and onto the bench and grabbed her by the wrist to keep her from running away.

"It's all right now," Longarm said, trying to soothe her. "He can't hurt you now. You're all right. Come with me, Sybil. I'll take you to your mama."

Instead of acquiescing, Sybil Nellis began slamming her fists against Longarm's chest and trying to kick him in the shins.

"You bastard, you. You killed Harry. You killed my man."

Chapter 54

"Let me go, you big ape." Sybil continued to try to hit Long-arm, battering his chest with her fists and stomping on his toes.

Finally he had had enough of her shit. He slapped her—hard, across the face—then turned her around and spanked her butt.

While he was so thoroughly occupied with Sybil, he was watching over her shoulder to see if the other brothers were going to come out after him, perhaps this time with guns.

"Settle down, damn you," he snapped at her. "What's the matter with you? Don't you *want* to be rescued?"

"No, you stupid shit. I wasn't kidnapped to begin with. Harry is my man. Was, I mean. We were going to be married someday. When we struck it rich," she bawled.

"What about your father and mother?" Longarm asked.

"Well what about them? My mother, the bitch, ran away. My father," she shrugged, "it wasn't Harry's fault what happened to my father."

"Do you mean you were with these bastards of your own free will?" Longarm said.

"Of course I was. Harry loved me. Really loved me. Oh, my parents used the word a lot, but they didn't know what love is, neither one of them. I'm surprised I was able to get born. I mean, I know my parents must have done it, but I can't imagine them doing that."

Longarm snorted. No kids, it seemed, could imagine their father in the saddle, rutting there between their mother's legs. It was something most kids could not visualize, did not *want* to see in their mind's eye.

Hell, Longarm himself could not imagine his father pounding his mother's belly like that, never mind that he knew it had to have been done.

Sybil Nellis was no different from anyone else in that regard.

But the little bitch's tiny fists felt hard as stones, and she kept on throwing them.

"Will you please calm down?" he said. He tried to be patient with her, but it was not easy. "Tell me what happened to your parents."

"Harry and Ross and George didn't mean anything by it. They just thought it would be fun to make like, um, like they were kidnapping me. But they really didn't. I mean, I wanted to come with them. Then we could all live off the land. You know, like the Indians used to do."

Longarm had heard bullshit stories before in his day. This, he thought, was one of them. "So how'd your father come to be dead and your mother scared half to death?"

"That was just . . . like an accident, sort of. My father came out of the tent all mad and giving orders like he always did, except Harry and the fellows didn't have to take his orders, and he snapped at them and so . . . and so they shot him."

"Which one did?" Longarm asked.

"All of them."

"And your mother?"

Sybil shrugged. "She ran away."

"Where are their guns now?" he asked.

The girl shrugged again.

"In there?" He hooked a thumb toward the entrance to their diggings.

At least the girl had settled down for the moment. But Longarm still kept his left hand clamped firmly around her wrist. And his eyes locked just as firmly on that hole where the brothers had disappeared.

"What did you do with your father's body?" he asked. He had not seen any signs of a grave anywhere near.

Another shrug. "They pitched him in the creek. I mean, it wasn't like he cared anymore. He floated downstream. I don't know what happened to it after that."

To "it" she had said, not "him." The faithless little bitch did not even care that much about her own father.

Some children, Longarm thought, should be drowned at birth. This was one of them.

"Let's go, Sybil," he said, tugging at her wrist.

"I'm not going anywhere with you. I'm staying right here with the boys. They'll take care of me."

"You are going with me to—"

He did not have time to finish the sentence, because the remaining two Carver brothers chose that moment to come out into the sunlight again.

Except this time the sledgehammers had been left inside, and they had rifles in their hands.

Chapter 55

Longarm dragged Sybil down out of the line of fire and dropped to the ground beside her.

Both brothers fired, their bullets sizzling over Longarm's head.

He already had his Colt in hand. It spat twice, then twice more. The brother on the left fell sprawling onto the rocky ledge of the diggings he had stolen from Frank Nellis. The brother on the right—Longarm had no idea which of them was which and at the moment did not really care—staggered but came on.

Longarm triggered his .45 again.

And got a metallic click in response. His five shots were gone, and he did not have time to reload. He let go of Sybil and sprang toward Carver, startling the man into a wild shot that did not even come close enough for Longarm to hear the bullet's passage.

Before the man had time to crank the lever and seat a fresh cartridge, Longarm was on him.

He wrenched the Winchester out of the man's hands and swung the rifle like a club. It caught Carver under the ear and knocked him off his feet.

He still had fight in him. He tried to come at Longarm,

driving up from his knees, only to be met by the butt of the Winchester. The wood of the stock splintered from the force of the impact. The blow probably broke Carver's jaw, but Longarm did not take time to investigate the damage that had been done.

He turned the rifle around, levered a cartridge into the chamber, and at point-blank range fired a .44-40 slug into Carver's chest. Then another just to be sure.

Finally he dropped the rifle and turned back to Sybil, who was making a run for the picket line where they had tied their horses and the mules that had belonged to her parents.

Longarm ran slipping and sliding down to the horses. He reached them at the same time as Sybil and once again grabbed for her.

The girl turned on him with a knife in her hand. Whether she had had it with her to begin with or snatched it up as she started to run he would never know.

He defended himself, acting virtually on instinct, grabbing her wrist and turning it back away from his body.

And into hers.

The knife jabbed deep into Sybil Nellis's belly.

Longarm had not intended any such thing, but the simple truth was that he did not regret it. It had been her life or his, and to his mind there was no conflict there. He had done what he had to do. The girl was responsible for her own actions, to live or to die by them.

In this instance, it was to die.

She did, however, die slowly and in agony. Longarm placed her on the mat she had shared with Harry Carver and sat with her for three days and two nights before she finally expired.

And good riddance to her was his private thought. Not that he would ever say that to the girl's mother, but it was true.

When she was gone, he buried her—a small gesture she

had denied her own father—close to the creek-side graves of the Carver boys, and planted a small marker to serve for all three of them.

Then he gathered up all the livestock and took them back to visit with Katherine Jennings for a few days.

He needed the rest, he told himself. After all, he was on vacation here.

Besides, maybe Kat could use some of the spare animals to haul supplies in while she studied the wildlife up here. Any she did not want to keep she could sell to help finance her dissertation.

The mare and burro had to be returned to Silver Plume, of course. He would deal with Jane Nellis then. Although just exactly what he would tell her . . . He could come up with something before the time came. Something other than the truth, of course, but something.

In the meantime . . . he smiled, thinking of Katherine and her wild, wicked ways. Who knew that not all academics were stuffy creatures, eh?

Watch for

LONGARM AND THE ARAPAHO HELLCATS

the 419th novel in the exciting LONGARM
series from Jove

Coming in October!

LONGARM

GIANT-SIZED ADVENTURE FROM AVENGING ANGEL LONGARM.

BY TABOR EVANS

penguin.com/actionwesterns

M456AS0812

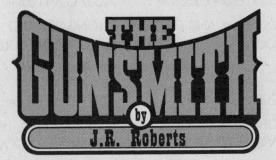